ELIZABETH CORRIGAN

I0638455

ANGEL IN THE DETAILS

BOOK FOUR: EARTHBOUND ANGELS

Angel in the Details: Book Four: Earthbound Angels
Copyright © 2019 by Elizabeth Corrigan. All rights reserved.

Paperback ISBN: 978-0-9862573-6-0
Ebook ISBN: 978-0-9862573-7-7

First Print Edition: October 2020

Cover and Formatting: Streetlight Graphics

For Julie, Bedlam's #1 fan

ANGELS AND DEMONS

Rank	Name	Virtue	Status
1	Lucifer (Satan, Sammael)	glory	demon
2	Michael	order	angel
3	Gabriel	joy	angel
4	Keziel	balance	angel
5	Uriel	death	angel
6	Sarakiel	courage	Dead
7	Lethe (Betzalel)	mercy	demon
8	Lilith (Lelial)	vengeance	demon
9	Mephistopheles (Baraquiel)	intelligence	demon
10	Siren (Zabethiel)	honesty	angel
11	Rachel	justice	angel
12	Nathaniel	faith	angel
13	Raziel	hope	Dead
14	Beelzebub (Asmodel)	generosity	demon
15	Raphael	innocence	angel
16	Sybil (Tzaphquiel)	patience	angel
17	Somniel	peace	angel
18	The Beast (Gaghiel)	tenacity	demon
19	Jophiel	service	angel
20	Azrael	love	dead
*	Bedlam (Azazel)	chaos	angel

CHAPTER 1

Michael

I SLASHED MY FLAMING GREATSWORD ACROSS the demon's chest. Had he been human, I would have cleaved his torso in two, but instead, he disappeared before my eyes. If I shifted into human form, I would no doubt see the inky darkness of his evil soul sucked into the nearest hellhole, but I remained as I was, and not because of the human onlookers. I couldn't care less about their meaningless stares. I simply didn't want the tangible proof that I couldn't see the hellholes, because Hell was barred to all angels.

Why should I be unable to go to Hell? I am the leader of the host of Heaven. Lucifer should have no domain I cannot defeat. I took a deep breath. I reminded myself I didn't want to go to Hell, but the thought that I could not go there stuck in my brain like a lightning-charged needle and would not leave. *I should be able to go to Hell. I should.*

I closed my eyes. I needed to make the thoughts stop. I counted to seven once, then twice, then seven times, but my old standby had no effect. *Only one thing makes the thoughts stop. One person. And I cannot go to her.* For eight thousand years I had treated her like the demon-spawn I thought she was, and she could never forgive me for that. Sometimes I could even convince myself her certain implacability was the true reason I stayed away, but I knew the truth. If I went to her side, I would never

1

leave. Stronger angels than I had fallen to her charm, and I needed to hold myself upright for Heaven.

For three months, I had focused on the only other thing that could distract me—sending demons to Hell where they belonged. The one I had just smote, one of Beelzebub's fiends, had been tempting children to steal from the marketplace in Dubai. I should know his name. It flickered on the tip of my tongue but would not spring to my mind. *I should know his name. He was an angel once. When they were angels, I knew all of their names.* My breath came more rapidly. *I can't follow them to Hell, and I can't know their names. I'm useless. Useless.*

Enough. I pulled my sword to me and pushed the spinning thoughts to the back of my mind. I focused outward, spreading my senses over the earth, looking for another demon to smite.

"Michael." A voice I did not want to hear broke my concentration. *Jophiel.* The small, blond angel was, for all practical sakes and purposes, my right hand man. *Which is wrong. Wrong, wrong, wrong.* Gabriel should have been my right hand angel, as he had been for thousands of years, until Cain lured him to earth. I had hated her for that, more even than I'd hated her for the evil in her mind and bones, but I couldn't hate her anymore. I could only wallow in shame at how I had treated her.

He needs something. Heaven needs something. I need to do something, to fix something, to be something. My heart pounded in my chest. I couldn't do it. I couldn't be the leader of the host at that moment, not until I pulled myself together.

Not until I kill more demons. "Not now, Jophiel." My voice came out gruff but steady. *Good.* I did not turn to look at him. I resumed my search for a demon. *Any demon.*

Listen to Jophiel. He needs you. You have responsibilities. Responsibilities that you are failing at again, again, again. My need to hunt demons clashed with my obligations to

Heaven, and the discordance disrupted my focus. I stood paralyzed, unable to listen to Jophiel and unable to search for a demon.

Find the demons. Listen to Jophiel. Find the demons. Listen to Jophiel. Find—

Jophiel shoved a small glass device into my face. It was one of those boxes humans spent all their time staring at. On the small screen, I saw an image of a tall, muscular man with dark hair and brilliant blue eyes use a flaming greatsword to turn a man to dust. *It's me.* I jerked back at the realization. *What am I doing in the tiny box?* "What is that?"

"It's a smartphone." Jophiel kept the device in my view, and the tiny copy of me destroyed another demon, then another. "Which you should know. You should familiarize yourself with the modern sources of evil in the world."

Smartphone. The word sounded familiar. I had certainly seen enough of the things, though as a general rule, I did not concern myself with humans. I worried about running Heaven, and demons and their evil. *And that's wrong. Heaven's job is to protect humans from the evil of demons. If they're creating their own evils, you should try to stop that, too. You should care. You should care. You should—*

"You're showing up all over the human news with this—this rampage!" Jophiel sounded outraged, like he was chastising me, but that couldn't be right. I was his boss. "For now they seem to think it's some kind of dramatic global theater event, but it won't be long before you expose all knowledge of angelkind to humans!"

Oh, Light. I'm ruining the secrecy of angels. My lungs couldn't fill with air, but I couldn't let Jophiel see that. "Maybe it's time they knew we existed. If they're creating evil such as these wisephones, they clearly need a more powerful guiding force."

"'Maybe it's time they knew we existed?'" Jophiel's voice dripped with more disdain than it should have, but

I let it pass. "We already get more prayers than we can handle. Imagine if people knew we were listening! Also imagining humans realizing that demons exist! Those miserable creatures would be lining up to sell their souls faster than you could say, 'Form a queue!'"

Is that right? Has humanity fallen so far? Have I failed that completely at my job of shepherding them? I didn't know. What I did know was that we should be able to answer more prayers now that I had put Gabriel in charge of the field angels when he had demanded it. *But you only did that to keep Gabriel tied to Heaven, not to help humanity. You were scared he was going to leave you for Cain again.*

Cain. Light, I wanted to see her. I wanted her calm presence to quiet the rampaging thoughts in my head. But I couldn't cave to the weakness of needing her, any more than I could listen to Jophiel continue his insolence. I squeezed my eyes shut and sought out a tainted soul.

A banshee wandered through the dark streets of London. Her silent screams of despair pierced my mind. All within earshot would glimpse despair, and some might be driven to desperate acts. I rushed forward to run her through with my sword. Banshees had little in the way of physical skills, so I anticipated an easy kill. Before I reached her, though, she focused her scream on me, and my doubts and insecurities, never far from the surface of my mind, threatened to overwhelm me.

I'm exposing angelkind. I'm going to overwhelm Heaven. I'm neglecting my duties. I'm longing for the company of a mortal girl. I'm letting Jophiel talk down to me. I'm a failure as a leader, a nothing of an angel. I can't lead as Lucifer did, and I'll never be able to. I'm a failure. I'm a failure. I'm—

My flaming greatsword clattered to the ground, and I couldn't move to pick it back up. The banshee, too waiflike to wield it, kicked it away. I struggled to focus on her and force my hands to grab her throat, but the futility of my existence overwhelmed me.

"Our old ruler forbade us to harm you," she whispered in my ear. "But we have a new leader now, thanks to you."

Lethe, I thought. *Lethe protected me.* Until recently, Lethe, my onetime lover, had ruled the banshees, and our eternal angel love had protected me from her despair. I had heard, though, that Lethe had abandoned her post, leaving it open for Sybil, one of the two seraphs I had damned three months ago. The other, Somniel, ruled the incubi and succubi.

Thinking about the hierarchies of Heaven and Hell steadied my mind some, and I dove for my sword. Before I could grab the hilt, the banshee screamed again, and I covered my ears in a futile attempt to shut out the mental assault. *Lethe. Cain. Sybil. Somniel. Jophiel.* All my failures swam before my eyes. I buried my head in my hands and felt to one knee.

The screaming continued. *I'm revealing my weakness to Hell, to everyone. If I were righteous enough, the banshee scream couldn't affect me. It's so hard to hide it since Cain... since Cain...*

"Michael!" I knew that voice, and while shortly ago it had annoyed me, I was now grateful it could pull me out of my fog. Jophiel pressed my sword into my hand, and its solid hilt steadied me. I had a connection to it. In fact, I realized, I could have called it back at any time. *I should have remembered that. I should have—*

I could not allow myself to focus on my despair. I gripped my sword by the hilt and slashed upward, forcing the flaming blade into the gut of the banshee. She disappeared into the mist, and I collapsed to my knees again and held the sword like a prayer.

Jophiel stood over me. I could feel his presence, but I did not open my eyes. "This is another reason you can't go on fighting demons," he said. "They're getting stronger. Two more seraphs have fallen, which has tilted the balance toward Hell." His voice held more than a note of accusation.   Without standing up, I gave him a look that reminded him which of us was the leader of the host. He paled and took a step backwards. "Michael, I didn't mean—"

"Are you saying I should not have condemned Sybil and Somniel?" I spoke softly and put a note of warning menace in my tone, hopefully covering the doubt in my heart. "They rebelled against Heaven. Some of the angels have still not recovered." Three months ago, Sybil and Somniel had knocked out all of Heaven's angels and tormented them with nightmares in a desperate bid to rid Heaven of the former demon Bedlam. Gabriel had managed to save Heaven, but some of the angels remained trapped in their own minds.

Jophiel swallowed and stood a bit straighter. "I just wanted to point out that the solution to all problems is not sending things to Hell. Sybil and Somniel's methods were flawed, but their hearts were in the right place. They tried to rid Heaven of a threat that needs to be acknowledged."

That you need to acknowledge. Did I? Was Bedlam a threat to Heaven? He had died to save another person—*Cain*—and God had lifted him back into the arms of Heaven. I could not deny the will of God. Of could I? Bedlam was anathema to me, chaos to my order, and I had seen no evidence that he planned to work for Heaven's greater good. His plan seemed to be to play the dilettante on Earth at Cain's side. Should I have lost two seraphs in defense of Bedlam? *In defense of Heaven. In defence of God. In defense of what is right.*

"Oh, great, now *I'm* on the news." Jophiel had the glass box out again. He shoved it back in my face. A fuzzy video showed Jophiel handing me my sword. At the bottom of the screen, red and yellow words read, "Does Heaven's Avenger have a sidekick?"

I turned in the direction the video had to have been taken from, and a curtain fell in a window. "Heaven's Avenger?"

"That's what they're calling you." Jophiel shook his fist at where the curtain had fallen. "I'm not his sidekick! I'm trying to stop him!"

I took the device from Jophiel and stared at it. The screen had gone black. "Make it play again," I said.

"I don't see how—"

"Make it play again." If there had been any doubt that the first time I said the words had been an order, there was no doubt in the second. Jophiel muttered under his breath, but after a few taps on the glass screen, he had the video back up. I saw myself fall to my knees at the banshee's inaudible scream. I beheld my own weak shudder as despair overwhelmed my mind. I watched Jophiel save me. When the fuzzy images cut off, after a second, they began again, and I stared at the whole thing again, and then a third time. I watched my weakness on display for the world to see.

I'm losing my mind, I thought. Three months ago, Cain had calmed the circling thoughts in my head, and since then, the only thing that brought me relief was smiting demons. I had started with one demon a week, but the pace had increased over time. If that little number at the bottom of the screen was a date and time, I had apparently been taking out demons non-stop for two days. *And it's still not enough.*

When the video started up a fourth time, Jophiel snatched the box back. "That's enough of that." He pressed the big button under the images, and I thought to use his distraction to go find another demon. *I just need to kill one more. Just one more, and maybe then I can go back and do my job. One more.*

He grabbed my arm. "Don't even think about disappearing on me again. I'm just going to follow you until you decide to stop this nonsense and run Heaven like you are supposed to."

I shook him off. "Do not forget to whom you speak. I am the leader of the host and your superior."

"Then act like it!"

Act like it. Act like it. Act like it. The words echoed through my mind, and I couldn't even process what they meant. What was my purpose? What did it even mean to lead the host? I wasn't sure anymore. *One more demon. I'll just destroy one more demon, and then I'll go back and figure it out.*

I stretched out my consciousness, and this time I found a demon I recognized. He was standing in a dark alley behind a bar in the midwestern United States. His perfectly chiseled features marked him as an incubus, but he was attractive even for his kind. Unsurprising, since he was also the most powerful of his kind. Word on the celestial pipeline indicated he had sought to lead the incubi and succubi after Azrael's death, but Lucifer refused to hand the position over to a cherub, even one as strong as the self-proclaimed Prince of Lies.

"Asphodel." I brandished my sword in his direction.

"Ugh, finally." Asphodel did not sound afraid in the slightest. "Do you have any idea how long I've been waiting in this disgusting alley for you to show your face?"

The last time I had thrust my blade through Asphodel's chest had been centuries ago. Apparently I needed to remind him how unpleasant it could be. I took a step forward, a growl rising in my throat.

Asphodel held up a finger and smiled. "Uh-uh-uh. I don't think you want to do that."

Something about his confidence set me on edge. "Why not?"

Something hard hit me on the back of the head, and as the ground rose up to meet my face, Asphodel's grin widened. "That's why."

CHAPTER 2

Siren

THE KATANA IN MY HANDS shone like moonlight against Heaven's gold, and the ribbed leather of the hilt chafed against my uncalloused palms. I had picked my form at the beginning of time, and smooth hands had seemed like a better idea before I experienced blisters from hours wielding a sword around a practice field. Rachel didn't ordinarily allow me to wield a light blade, but we were playing for keeps.

A warrior angel strode up to me in what seemed like slow motion. I considered closing my eyes to prove I didn't need to see her to parry her clumsy blows, but I decided against it. I could not allow my arrogance to cost me this battle. One tap from the longsword in her hand, and I would be as unconscious as the slew of warriors at my feet. Rachel would never allow me to join their ranks.

Whoosh. The warrior's blade sliced toward me, and I dodged it by a foot or more. With a swish of my own weapon, I returned the blow, but my strike landed true, and the angel fell at my feet. I heard rather than saw the next assailant attempt to land what I certainly hoped was a dagger in my back, and the downswing of my sword hit her as I pivoted away from the blow.

The next warrior came up on the other side of the body, clearly hoping to slow me down or trip me up at having to go around or over the angel. He certainly did not expect me to kick her unconscious form toward him. If he had, he probably wouldn't have stumbled and fallen on his own blade. A collective gasp came from the choir of warrior angels waiting for their turn to take me on. I hoped their strategy was to make me feel guilty for using their—and hopefully soon *my*—comrade in such a manner. More likely they were simply appalled. Either way, I ignored their shock. I was the angel of truth, not dignity.

From the slower steps of my next target, I ascertained that my gambit had created a secondary effect of unnerving my temporary adversaries. I shoved down a wave of disappointment. Angels should know better than anyone that all's fair in war. Humans said "love and war," but they were idiots. There was nothing fair about angel love.

I lost count of how many warriors sprinted at me. I cut them all down before they could hit me, and they landed at my feet. The pile of angels impeded my footwork some, but not nearly as much as it did theirs. If I was completely honest—and I always was—their easy defeat disappointed me. A tiny, ugly thing like me shouldn't be able to take down Heaven's greatest warriors without breaking a sweat.

All at once, after a final bloodless swipe of gold and moonlight, they stopped coming. I looked up and saw one person left standing in the training room. Rachel, Heaven's own warrior princess—not that she would call herself anything so foolish—stood alone before me. Her white robe hung open to reveal her full plate armor, which I would be a fool to think her anything but fully mobile in. I looked past her beautiful face and chestnut brown hair into the truth of her soul: She was never going to let me join the warriors.

I took down her entire cadre! my mind protested. *I can fight circles around anyone else Heaven has to offer.* Looking into her blue eyes, I realized my skills didn't matter. She had nothing but disdain for me. Rage overtook me as I marched out of the sea of angel bodies toward her.

I can show her. If I take her down, she'll have to let me in. If Michael hears about it, he'll put me in charge of the warriors, and she can be my second in command.

I raised my katana to meet her greatsword. My instincts screamed at me to slash and grab, take her out as quickly as I had her minions, but a cooler, calmer part of me took over. *Rachel won't be as easy to fight as her minions. Odds are good she keeps them only half-trained to her own ego. Wait. She's not going to let you in anyway. Someday you may really need to fight her, and you're going to need every advantage you can get. Like her thinking you're weak.*

When she slashed and pushed with her greatsword, I fell back. I made a hard enough strike with my katana that she would think I was using my full strength, but I held back, and I retreated. I made as if to get around her defenses but let her block me. My foot hit an angel body I was well aware was immediately behind me, and I pretended to stumble. I stumbled to my knees. "I yield." I couldn't make my voice sound anything but bitter as I spat the words at her greaves.

Rachel's petite features twisted into a sneer. "Honestly, Siren, I thought maybe you had something in you with how quickly you bested my warriors, but apparently I just need to train them harder. We're done here."

I glared up at her for all I was worth. "You dare to all but lie in my presence. You were never going to let me in!"

Rachel turned her back on me and strode to the weapon rack to put her greatsword away. "Of course I wasn't. My warriors must be of unimpeachable character, and you are the least trustworthy of Heaven's angels."

"Least trustworthy?" I dug the katana into the solid ground beneath the gold mist and used the blade to push myself up. I would never do such a thing with my own weapon, but I didn't care about denting Rachel's, if it even could be dented. "You're saying the angel of *truth* is untrustworthy?"

Rachel dropped her greatsword into the weapon rack with a *thunk*. "You're right. Untrustworthy is unfair. You've never been disloyal. But look at your compatriots. The Grigori all died or fell. Your subsequent companions betrayed Heaven while you were off cavorting with that demon who calls himself an angel. You manage to make it out of all these incidents unscathed, which means you're either innocent or the greatest mastermind in Heaven or Hell. Either way, something about you corrupts others, and I will not have it in my ranks."

Pick up that sword and say that again, I wanted to say. I had watched her fight for ten thousand years, and I was pretty sure I could take her out if I tried. I took a deep breath. Humans said wisdom was the better part of valor, and even though there was no angel of wisdom, and valor was a demon, I heeded their advice. I took deep breaths as I walked over to the weapon rack and returned the katana to its place.

Only after I had left the training room did I realize what I had done. I had feigned and feinted and pretended to be something entirely other than what I was. Yet another of the human aphorisms that seemed to be my lot ran through my head: Actions speak louder than words. With my actions, I had done the impossible. I had lied.

"I don't like sprinkles! They're pretty and colorful, but they don't taste like anything, and if they're cold, they stick to the roof of my mouth. My favorite fairy tale is Beauty and the Beast, despite the Stockholm Syndrome elements. Please don't yell at me."

I buried my face in my hands. Concerned my powers were fading, I'd sought out the only angel who had less to do than I did and asked him to lie in my presence. Not only were my powers in full force, Raphael's truths were starting to rot my brain.

"Okay, enough." I tried to keep the testiness out of my voice, but I failed. "My power is still working. So why...?"

"Why what?" Raphael pulled on a string of his curly red hair. When I didn't answer, he shrugged. "Can I stop trying to lie to you now? Everyone tells me I'm a terrible liar anyway."

"I don't care if I believe you," I said. "I care if you can make the words come out." He had a point, though. Maybe only subtle lies could get past my power. Or maybe I was wasting my time. Maybe my ability to lie with actions was like the sarcasm loophole. I didn't like it, though. I hadn't liked anything in my life since Sybil and Somniel had fallen. *As they deserved.* I hadn't liked anything in my life before that either, but things had gotten so much worse since their betrayal. The other angels looked at me like I might sprout horns and light Heaven on fire at any moment, and Keziel wouldn't even let me into her new coma ward for the angels who didn't recover from the attack. *Though that may have more to do with my snide comments about the handmaidens finally having something useful to do than with Keziel not trusting me.*

I hated my fellow angels. I thought they were useless and short-sighted and so wrapped up in following their ridiculous procedures that they didn't do anything useful. Still, I couldn't lie to myself. I hated them, but I also needed them. Without them, I was lonely as Hell, and from what Mephistopheles had told me in some of his more drunken moments, Hell could get pretty damn lonely.

I also loathed being so useless. I hadn't had a job before, but when I'd made recommendations, I'd had the weight of Sybil and Somniel behind me. Heaven seemed to have long forgotten that Sybil and Somniel were actually my keepers, assigned to me after the whole Grigori incident to make sure I didn't stray from the path of righteousness as my fellows had. The other angels thought the traitors had been my friends, or possibly even my followers, and

I had fed into that belief to help my own status. *Which, come to think of it, is another kind of lie.* The truth that was supposed to be the center of my essence had a crack down the middle, and I had no idea what to do about it.

"Raphael, how do you deal with not having a job?" I asked. He never seemed to have any friends or purpose, yet he was happy as a proverbial clam, humming some nursery song and playing with a bit of the fluff of gold that made up Heaven's floor.

"I have a job," he said in between hums.

"What?" I gaped at him. "No, you don't." *Can't lie in my presence.* "What do you do?"

Raphael stared at the mist in his hands until it turned into the shape of a duck, then blew on it until it scattered back into the air. "Oh, I wander around Earth looking for things that are out of place and report them to Michael."

"So, you're a field angel?"

He lifted a new bit of fluff and willed it into a lamb. "No, they report to Jophiel. Or I guess Gabriel now. I report directly to Michael."

Wandering around the world to see if anything was out of place didn't seem like much of a job. Jophiel had a whole system in place for monitoring humans' affairs. Whether his system actually helped anything was another matter, but Michael never showed any awareness of Jophiel's failings. More likely Michael had given Raphael the "duty" to keep him busy. I wished I were idiotic enough to believe some bullshit job was crucial to Heaven's oversight.

No, not idiotic. That's not... well, it's true, but it's not fair. You want angels to like you, so you need to stop thinking of them as idiots. Raphael is blithe and trusting and other good things that lead to believing bullshit. He's not idiotic. I was so busy policing my own thoughts, I almost missed what Raphael had said. "Wait. Gabriel is in charge of the field angels now?"

"Yup." Raphael hummed a different song. "Michael told him he could after the attack on Heaven."

I couldn't believe I hadn't heard about this. Surely if Gabriel was trying to organize the field angels, I would have heard about it. "Raph, has Gabriel *met* the field angels?"

Raphael shrugged. "He must have. How could he be in charge of them if he hadn't?"

"How indeed." I could not imagine a situation under which Jophiel would introduce Gabriel to the field angels. *Which means Gabriel's either forming his own task force, or Jophiel's been running him in circles for three months. Either way, he needs me.*

"I gotta go." I pushed myself to my feet.

"Bye, Siren!" Raphael gave me an idyllic-not-idiotic smile.

I found Gabriel in the receiving room, standing on his own. Despite his archangel status, he wasn't much more trusted in Heaven than I was. He had spent two thousand years on Earth and had fallen in love with a human. Our mutual alienation should have made us the perfect pair, but I resented him for neglecting his duties for so long, and he blamed my annual drunkenness for Azrael nearly killing his girlfriend. That I'd also helped save her was apparently irrelevant. Nonetheless, he had more clout than I did, and I planned to extort both that fact and my knowledge to get myself a job.

I held my head up and strode over to him. "Gabriel—"

"Do you know where Michael is?" Gabriel asked, not taking in my determined stance.

As I looked at him, I realized he appeared distracted. *Probably because he's frustrated with not being able to work with the field angels. I can help him there.* "Not since the meeting two days ago, but Gabriel—"

"I can't find him anywhere. I'm getting really worried."

Michael, missing? The thought knocked my goal to the back of my mind. Michael wasn't my favorite angel by any stretch of the imagination, especially lately. He used to at least pretend to listen to me, but lately when I spoke, he stared blankly at a spot over my shoulder and waited for me to finish. I tried to point out that it wasn't fair of him to blame me for Sybil and Somniel's malfeasance when he had assigned them to me, and he'd walked out on me. I had nearly cried at his complete rejection, and I hated myself for that.

Still, I didn't want anything bad to happen to him. *Relax,* I told myself. *This is Gabriel, who's only got two watts on Raphael at most. He probably hasn't done a proper search.* "Did you ask Jophiel?" I did not add "Because he's got his head so far up Michael's ass it's impossible to find one without the other. *See? Progress! I can be diplomatic.*

Gabriel muttered something about Jophiel being the least helpful angel he had ever met. I think I even heard a swear word in there. I gaped at him. Gabriel usually spoke with all the kindness and diplomacy I lacked, even in my presence. "Pardon me?"

Gabriel sighed, clearly feeling guilty for his words. "Jophiel said something about not being Michael's keeper and hurried me along."

So much was wrong with that one sentence. For one, Jophiel always knew where Michael was, and the fact that he either didn't know or was concealing it was problematic. For another "keeper" was a loaded term for those of us with Biblical ties, and I didn't like the implications. Finally, Jophiel shouldn't be able to order Gabriel around. The fact that he could was good news for me, because it meant he probably did need me to introduce him to the field angels. All in all, Jophiel's evasion was bad news from Heaven, and contrary to popular belief, I wanted Heaven to keep functioning.

"That's not suspicious or anything," I said.

Gabriel waved a hand. "I think it was a dig at me. You know, because Cain and I..." He trailed off, apparently not wanting to give voice to his relationship with the Bible's most notorious murderer, even if the Old Testament got things wrong.

I considered this. "So you think he knows where Michael is and won't tell you? That's pretty fucked up."

Gabriel rubbed the bridge of his nose, a gesture so reminiscent of Michael I nearly laughed. Heaven had a way of piling frustrations on its leaders. I managed about thirty seconds of sympathy before the snide part of my mind reminded me the archangels would have less stress if either of them had any management skills.

"I need Jophiel to transfer operations of the field angels to me," said Gabriel. "It's been three months, and I've gotten nothing out of him. I don't know who the field angels are or what the process to transfer prayers to them is. I'm at my wit's end, and I need Michael to intervene. Jophiel knows this, so he won't tell me where Michael is." Gabriel looked at me and cringed, as if he suddenly realized who he was talking to. People couldn't lie around me, but they weren't forced to expel all their truths. Nonetheless, honesty had a way of snowballing once it got started.

"Actually, that's what I wanted to talk to you about."

"Oh?"

I stood up as straight as I could, given my tiny stature, and tried to speak with authority. "I can introduce you to the field angels."

"You can?" Gabriel's voice sounded both skeptical and hopeful.

"Can't lie, remember?"

Gabriel considered me. "Siren, every other seraph, Michale included, has told me that only Jophiel can give me the information I need. How am I supposed to believe you can help me and they can't?"

17

Only because they pay zero attention to what Jophiel's doing. "Two possible reasons. The most likely is they don't have the info. But me? I'm Heaven's outsider. I don't have a job. I don't have a purpose. I wander Heaven and Earth finding out secrets other people don't want me to have."

"That doesn't sound very honest."

Don't you dare judge me! I wanted to say, but I kept my voice light. "What's more honest than ferreting out secrets and bringing them into the light?"

"Okay, then. Tell me. Who are the field angels?"

"I will, on one condition."

Gabriel blanched. "You want payment?"

"I want a job!" The way he said the word "payment" made my wishes sound so cheap and tawdry, and he was right. I wanted Heaven and the field angels to function, and giving Gabriel the information he needed would help that. Holding out for my own self-interest was wrong, and yet I had to do it. "If I tell you who the field angels are, I want to be second in command."

Gabriel let out a bark of laughter. "You want to work for me? After what happened with Cassia? You think for one second I would trust you again?"

"Yes!" I wanted to rip my own hair out. "Cassia's fine. I made sure of that. And I'm willing to give you information no one else will. That has to make you trust me a little bit." I hated the desperation in my voice, but I kept going. "Please, Gabriel, I just want a job. I want to do something that's actually useful to Heaven. I want to help!"

"Help who, Siren? Yourself? I've never known you to have a good thing to say about anyone, human or angel."

"Hey, just because I judge humans for their terrible decisions does not mean I will not defend to the death their right to free will."

Gabriel studied me for a long moment, and I was certain when he opened his mouth, he would tell me to get lost.

18

"I'll tell you what. If you introduce me to the field angels, I will evaluate whether there's a place for you on the team."

I wanted to protest, but the glint in his ordinarily placid blue eyes told me this was the best I was going to get out of him. "Fine," I said.

Gabriel gave a perfunctory nod. "I have something else I need to do first, but I'll meet you on Earth in a couple of hours. I assume the field angels are down there?"

"You assume correctly. They don't put in a lot of appearances up here these days."

"Except to get their missions, of course." Fortunately Gabriel walked away at that point. I couldn't think of an honest way to agree with his statement. I kept pace with him as he approached the passage to Earth, and when he reached the orifice, he turned back to me. "Wait. You said there were two reasons the seraphim might not tell me about the field angels. What was the second?"

I gave him my sweetest smile. "Oh, that they might not want to tell you. I said I'd introduce you to the field angels, and I will, but Gabriel, you're not going to like it."

CHAPTER 3

Bedlam

"I CAN'T BELIEVE I LET YOU drag me to a frat party."

Surprised at the menace in Khet's voice, I glanced over at her.her. She looked pretty in an olive green dress that set off tiny flecks of color in her brown eyes. She had put on make-up for the occasion and curled her black hair, but her scowl as she gazed up at the white-columned house ruined the effect.

"Come on, Khet!" I bounced on my toes, as much to keep warm in the cold Maryland-in-December air as to encourage her with my excitement. ."It's an end-of-semester holiday blowout! You can't miss it! It's part of the whole college experience you wanted!"

Khet ran her fingers through her hair. "I wanted a college education, not whatever part of the experience came with crowds of people drinking and groping each other."

She was going to turn on her heel and go home. I knew it. So I threw my arm over her shoulder and eased her toward the loud hip-hop music coming out of the house. "Okay, so you don't like large gatherings, but this is a happy crowd! You'll get so caught up in everyone's cheer, you'll forget you didn't want to be here. Besides, there's music, and that means dancing. You don't want to miss out on the dancing."

Khet seemed unconvinced. "You're not just going because of Shannon, are you?"

I racked my brain trying to think if I knew a Shannon. Then I remembered I didn't know any humans who weren't Khet and stopped wasting my precious mental resources. "Who's Shannon?"

"Pretty blond girl who invited you to the party this afternoon? You told her you wouldn't miss it for the world, and she specifically said she would look for you?"

Did I?

Maybe? I mean, someone must have invited us or we wouldn't be coming.

Khet seems very concerned about this.

I cannot for the life of me imagine why.

"Why would I go to a party for a girl I met this afternoon?"

Khet rubbed her hand across the bridge of her nose. "She's in my literature study group. She's been over to the apartment like five times, and she always makes a point to talk to you. You really don't remember her?"

I shrugged. "If I say I do, can we go to the party?"

For some reason, my question made Khet relax. "Okay. Just don't stray too far from me tonight. I need you to block the voices."

"Sure thing!" I bounced a few steps ahead of her. I couldn't read minds like she could, but I was sure she was smiling.

Because it had taken me so long to get her out of the apartment, the party was already in full swing. Someone shoved red Solo cups into our hands as soon as we walked in the door. Khet took one sniff of the beer inside, made a face, and set her drink on the nearest table. I, on the other hand, embraced the full college experience of cheap beer and downed the noxious substance in a few gulps.

"Come on! Let's dance!" I grabbed Khet's hand and dragged her into the room with what I had to concede was a very impressive sound system. Only a few people were dancing, but I'd never had a problem with social inhibitions. Under most circumstances, I'd have taken this opportunity to show off my stellar dance moves—Khet and I had been dancing together for years, and we knew how to impress a crowd. But when she started bopping inexpertly to the music like an average college girl, I had mercy on her and did the same.

Within an hour, the cheer of the party had infected her, as I'd known it would. "I can't believe I passed my first semester of college!" she said as we—or at least I—stopped for a drink break. "Other people keep thinking it, and I keep realizing it's true of me too!"

"Here's to you!" I held up my cup, though when I went to take a drink, I realized it was empty.

"Isn't that, like, your fourth beer?" Khet asked as I refilled my cup.

"Um…" I tried to count back to how many I had drunk, but my brain had a hard time remembering. She was probably right, if I couldn't even count to four. "I'm fine. It's not like angels are lightweights."

"Okay, but this is your official warning that if you so much as think about doing a keg stand, I will drag you out of here."

I stuck my tongue out at her. "You're no fun."

She laughed. "Well, even though you're the one consuming all the liquids, I'm the one who has to use the bathroom. I'll be back in a minute. Don't do anything I wouldn't do."

"Okay. I promise to only meddle in other people's affairs and get myself shot and killed while you're gone."

"Touche." She gave me one last grin then disappeared into the crowd. I shuffled my feet a bit in time to a Kelly Clarkson song as I finished my beer.

I hate this song. I should change it.

Mmm. Bad idea. Khet would get upset.

How would she know?

She can read minds, remember?

I moved to refill my cup when a college girl with blond ringlets appeared in front of me. "OMG, you came!" I tried not to think of piglets as she squealed, but it was hard.

I tried to place her heart-shaped face and dainty freckles. Nothing was coming to mind, so I dredged up the name Khet had mentioned at the beginning of the party. "Shannon? Of course I came. You invited me, didn't you?"

She giggled. Somehow that still made me think of piglets. "Yeah, but I didn't think Chloe would let you come. She's such a stick-in-the-mud."

For some reason, I found that hysterical. "Believe me, she's not," I said between laughs. "I have met some epic sticks-in-the-mud, and she doesn't even come close."

"Yeah, I saw you guys dancing," said Shannon. "But Chloe says she has a different boyfriend."

"Yeah, Gabriel," I said, surprised at the distaste in my voice. "But Gabs isn't a big party-goer. Or a big college-goer. So you're unlikely to meet him."

"You don't go to college either, but I see you." My brain was trying to throw out a warning sign at her tone, but I couldn't place why. "Did you graduate already?"

"Light, no! You wouldn't catch me in school for all the groundhogs in Punxsutawney."

"So what do you do?" Shannon wrinkled her nose. "Work?'

I laughed, probably too loudly. "Most assuredly not. Khet will tell you I'm the laziest person she's ever met, and she's met a *lot* of people."

Shannon's face scrunched up even further. "Why do you call her Khet when her name is Chloe?"

The truth was on the tip of my tongue, but I pulled it back in time. Lying wasn't something I bothered with under the best circumstances, and Khet was right that I'd had a bit too much to drink. I was sober enough to remember the fires and pictchforks and gunshot wounds that came with the truth getting out, though. "I've known her for a long time. Khet's a nickname."

I expected her to press me more, but she didn't seem all that interested in Khet's name. "So you're, like, a trust fund baby or something?"

"Or something." I wondered if she was too young to get a Kato Kaelin reference.

"Well, I think you should come to school," she said. "I'd help you out with your classes."

I let out a noise halfway between a snort and a guffaw. *When is Khet coming back?* "Why would you do that?"

A slow smile crept over Shannon's face. "Hm. Maybe you're right. Maybe you're too dumb for school. But that's okay. I like you anyway." Then, as if in slow motion I was somehow powerless to stop, she snaked her hands around my neck and pulled me down into a kiss.

What are you doing? Stop her! She's a barely legal girl who probably doesn't know who Kato Kaelin is and definitely can't fathom the entirety of your existence.

But it's been so. Damn. Long.

This is about Keziel, isn't it? I thought you were done with things being about Keziel.

Shut the fuck up.

To my surprise, my brain did shut up, and I let myself take a moment to appreciate the warmth of Shannon's mouth on mine, the delightful tickle of her finger twirling the hair at the base on my neck, and the electric feel of her tongue meeting mine.

When I pulled away, I probably should have looked at Shannon or listened to what she was saying, but a force greater than I was drew my gaze over her shoulder. Suddenly, all I could see was Khet's face over Shannon's shoulder. I was pretty good at reading my best friend's expression, but I couldn't tell what she was feeling at that moment. When she turned on her heel and headed toward the entrance of the frat house, I knew I needed to follow her. I all but shoved Shannon out of the way and pushed through the crowd to get to Khet.

I caught up to her on the edge of the porch and grabbed her arm. "Khet!"

She whirled around to face me, and when she hissed at me, I couldn't tell if she was angry or just didn't want to be overheard. "I'm not doing this."

I knew I should match her tone, but I was tipsy and frustrated. I flung out my hands and said in a voice anyone could hear, "You're not doing what?"

"You told me you didn't come to see Shannon." Her still-quiet voice held an accusation.

"I didn't! She found me! We were talking and then, well, she kissed me."

"You can't do that!"

"What do you mean, I can't do that? I can kiss whoever I want. You don't get to tell me I can't."

Why are we having this argument? I didn't want to kiss Shannon anyway.

I'm not the one who started it!

"Don't you see, Bedlam? You can't just go kissing whoever you want. You're free of Keziel for now, but if you fall in love with someone else, you're stuck again. You can't get attached to a human girl who's going to die!"

I sucked in a breath, and my mind tore in half. Part of me wanted to rip into her for thinking she could control my mistakes and decisions like that, but the rest of me knew I had been worried about the same thing. I could tell her I wasn't going to fall in love with Shannon—that much was probably true—but I couldn't promise the next random girl to come along wouldn't manage to steal my heart. Falling in love with a human stranger was exactly the kind of stupid thing I would do.

All the anger drained out of me. "Khet, I—"

"Hey, look! Chloe and Bedlam are under the mistletoe!"

Who's Chloe?

How does this random frat guy know my name?

And what's that about—?

I looked up to see a sprig of pointy leaves and white berries hung on the edge of the porch.

Mistletoe.

Khet looked down from the treacherous plant at the same time I did, and in sync we turned our heads to look at the strangers staring back at us. Before Khet could say anything—and before I could decide if this was a good idea—I leaned forward and kissed Khet. I told myself I didn't want a repeat of the incident inside, so I made sure to grasp Khet's arms so they were held tight to her side. In reality, I didn't want to know whether she would wind her arms around my neck and kiss me back or push me away.

Her mouth opened under mine, and I could feel the pressure of her lips responding. She was kissing me back—which gave me a brilliant idea. I couldn't fall in love with an average human. That way lay madness and desperation. I'd also be damned again before I got involved with an angel. *But Khet...*

Wouldn't it be perfect if I fell in love with Khet? She was my best friend, my confidante, my dance partner, and my salvation. She was the person I always came back to and the only person I wanted around. Without her I was nothing but a run-of-the-mill demon.

What about Gabriel?

What about Gabriel?

She loves him, and if she breaks up with him, he'll know the eternity of misery you've put up with from Keziel.

I think you're forgetting what's really important here. Namely, me.

I broke the kiss. "Do you want to get out of here?' I whispered. I might have imagined it, but I thought she trembled as she nodded.

We walked down the road in silence, standing close enough that our hands could have brushed as we moved but didn't quite. I kept glancing at her out of the corner of my eye, trying to read her expression. As we rounded the corner to her block, I remembered I could turn on my Azrael power—my ability to see who people loved. When I'd originally received the power upon Azrael's death, I hadn't been able to turn it off. Eventually, though, it had gotten annoying to see twice as many people everywhere I went, so I'd manufactured a mental off switch. I turned it on and looked at Khet again. Unsurprisingly, a shadowy, stoic Gabriel walked beside her, but I felt like his presence was dimmer than the last time I saw him. I could also make out the hint of another shape at her side.

Is it me? Maybe I wouldn't be able to tell. Khet says her power didn't let her know that Gabriel loved her.

That's ridiculous. You could see yourself next to Keziel all the time.

But I knew Keziel loved me. This is one of those weird nebulous situations.

You could try talking to her.

That sounds like a terrible idea. Talking about feelings. Ick.

I had a much better plan. I would wait until we were alone in her house, with no people staring, no mistletoe, and no other outside pressures, and then I would kiss her and see how she responded. She would probably want to have a whole big conversation after that, but I could teleport away.

She entered her apartment, which at this hour of night was almost pitch black, though I could still make out our shapes in the dim light that came in through the windows. She reached for the light, but I tugged her arm away and turned her toward me. I leaned forward, relishing this moment in which I finally got my life back on track.

A light turned on across the room. I held up my hand to block the glare that assaulted my eyes. Khet had already ducked out from under my arm and was moving toward the being responsible for my current blindness.

"Why are you guys standing in the dark?" asked Gabriel.

Khet threw herself into his embrace, but he seemed content to hug her. At least I didn't have to watch her kiss him instead of me. "We just got home," she said. "We were at a frat party. I didn't know you were coming, or I definitely would have stayed home." She kept her gaze fixed on Gabriel, but the glower in her voice was all for me.

"That's why all the..." Gabriel gestured at Khet's face and its unaccustomed level of makeup.

"Yeah, I thought I'd try to look nice." She laughed. "But it gets all over everything, so you don't want to kiss me right now."

Oh. That's why she didn't kiss him.

Not because she wanted to be kissing me instead? This is dashing all my dreams.

Really?

Yes.

"It's no problem." Gabriel's voice held a chuckle, which surprised me. He wasn't a big laugher. "I'm actually here to see Bedlam."

"Oh." Khet's shoulders sagged, and I focused so much on her disappointment, I almost missed the cause of her disappointment.

What? He wants to see me? Why? He never wants to see me.

I don't know. Maybe you should ask him.

Ehhhhhhhhhhh.

Why are you avoiding so many conversations today? You usually love talking.

"Can you leave us alone for a minute?" Gabriel asked Khet.

She arched her eyebrows halfway to her hairline, and the frown that had only been in her voice appeared on her face. "Okay."

It's not okay.

Not even a little bit.

Gabriel had the decency to look apologetic. "It's just... Heaven's business."

"No, it's fine," she said, though it was no more fine than it was okay. Whether or not Gabriel knew that was a different question. Even I could not match Gabriel's occasional willful cluelessness. "I'll go clean this goop off my face, and you guys can have your special Heavenly talk." She didn't glance back at either of us as she left.

I flopped down on the striped futon and reached for the remote. "What's up?"

"Do not even think about turning on the television." Gabriel grabbed the remote out of my hand. "This is serious. Michael's missing."

I was about to complain that I could listen to him and watch bad holiday movies at the same time—which I couldn't—but he'd actually managed to catch my attention.

"Ooo! Do you think Jophiel finally killed him in some kind of power coup? Or maybe Raphael accidentally killed him and hid the body somewhere! Alternatively, he could have realized he was a self-righteous prat and impaled himself on his own sword."

"I don't know what happened." Gabriel paced behind the futon. "I think Jophiel was the last one to see him, but he's not talking. I've scanned all of Heaven and Earth, and I can't find him anywhere. I can't scan the Haven, but I've asked around, and they haven't seen him in weeks. Either they've all gone evil, or he's not there."

"This adds weight to my 'stabbed himself' theory. Maybe he's in Hell."

"That seems really unlikely."

"So what do you want me to do?" I put my feet up on the coffee table. "Throw a party? Compose an epic in honor of his death?"

Gabriel looked appalled. "Of course not! I want you to find him!"

"How in the Realms am I supposed to find him?" I asked. "I don't have any magical finding people powers, and I can't go to Hell. If you want someone to check there, you shouldn't have chased Khet out of here so fast."

"I am not sending Cassia to Hell!" Gabriel's voice rose to a volume she could probably hear, and I half-expected her to stick her head out, but she didn't. Gabriel's next words were quieter. "I don't think he's in Hell. At least, I hope he's not. And you do have special powers. You have inherited Azrael's power. You can see who people love."

"I don't see how that can help. Michael and Lethe OTP and all, but I knew that before I had my power."

Gabriel pressed on despite having no idea what I had just said. "Maybe if you find Lethe and see the illusory Michael, it will give you a link to the real Michael. It's my only hope at this point."

"I'm pretty sure the power doesn't work that way."

Gabriel flung his hands up into the air. "Could you at least try?"

"Well, not at the moment. The only person around is you, and I already know where Khet is. Unless she crawled out the window out of frustration with us."

"Why would she be frustrated? Did you do something?"

Such a question.

Such a clueless idiot.

Him or me?

Ummmmm. I plead the fifth.

"Okay, fine. I will try your crazy scheme. I will go deal with the psycho demon who's trying—and probably failing—to be good, and hopefully this will somehow lead to finding my mortal enemy. It'll be great."

Gabriel's face relaxed as if a great weight had been taken off his shoulders. "Thanks, Bedlam. I knew I could count on you." He got a beatific look on his face, as if he were about to disappear.

"Wait a minute. Aren't you coming?" I asked.

Also, when did I become someone he could count on?

Especially to go on a secret mission to find Michael.

"I can't," said Gabriel. "I've finally—finally—got a lead on the field angels, and I can't pass this up without telling everyone Michael is missing. Which reminds me, please don't tell anyone about this. Not even Cassia. I can't imagine what would happen if the demons found out Michael was missing."

I grumbled an assent, even though I hated keeping secrets. "I hope you don't think that Khet deals with demons. I thought we were past that."

"Cassia deals with everything. It's who she is." At least he wore a fond smile on his face as he blinked out.

Gabriel's little mission to find Michael was putting a serious crimp in my plans to convince Khet we belonged together. In theory all I had to do was teleport to Lethe, find out illusory Michael was not linked to real Michael, and come home. But now that Gabriel apparently trusted me, if I did this task with any degree of success, I'd get assigned other Heavenly duties.

What I need is a way to prove to Gabriel I'm incompetent while simultaneously showing Khet we're perfect for each other.

You could just... not do what Gabriel asked.

Nah, too obvious.

"Hey, Khet!" I called.

She popped her head out of her bedroom. Her face was now makeup free, and she was toweling her hair. "What? Is he gone? Did he seriously not even stick around to say good-bye?'

She rarely expressed annoyance with Gabriel to me, which meant she had to be really annoyed. All to the good, so far as I was concerned. I gave her a broad smile. "Up for a road trip?"

CHAPTER 4

Michael

MY HEAD THROBBED WHEN I awoke. Before I could process where I was or even why I had been asleep, I followed my instinct to blink out of my pained human form. When my head didn't stop hurting because I, in fact, still had a head, I realized something was very wrong.

What happened? Did I break the part of me that teleports? Is that the part of my head that aches? Did someone remove it when I was unconscious? Is that even possible?

Calm down, I told myself, trying to take steady breaths. *Maybe you couldn't dematerialize because you were still dreaming.* When only a slight tremor remained in my chest, I tried once more to teleport, and when it didn't work, I had to open my mouth to make myself breathe.

Stay calm. I put all the command of the Leader of the Host into the thought, but my inner panic had always been more than a match for it. *Open your eyes. Figure out where you are. Then you can consider next steps.*

I opened my eyes. At least, I thought I did, but the darkness in front of me didn't change. I blinked and blinked again, but I still couldn't see anything but black. *Is this Hell? Am I in Hell?* Even with my mouth open, I couldn't catch a breath, and I probably would have entered into a full scale panic had a flame not appeared to my left.

"Ah, I see you're awake." The voice that accompanied the fire echoed through the cavernous chamber. The torch only let me see ten feet in any direction, but I could tell I was in a cave. I couldn't distinguish the color of the craggy stone floor in the firelight, but since I could see, I could also recognize the smell of wet stone and the sound of trickling water. I twisted toward the voice and took a menacing step forward.

I didn't make it more than a few inches before I felt the restraints on my wrists. Heavy iron cuffs covered half of my lower arms, and chains connected the restraints to the wall. I tugged at the chain with a sharp motion, which was enough to establish I probably couldn't remove the structure from the wall.

With a growl, I focused on the speaker who had lit the torch. Memories of how I had lost consciousness surfaced as I found Asphodel leaning against a rock to my left. His black eyes gleamed with devilish intent, and a malicious grin graced his handsome face. "Rise and shine, sleepyhead!" he said. "Welcome to my temporary kingdom. Temporary for me, that is. I have it on loan from Lucifer. You'll be here quite permanently, I'm afraid."

I called for my flaming sword, certain it could cut through these chains, but it did not come. I tried again to pull at the chains binding my wrists, and the resulting pain in my wrists lessened the pain in my head. "You misbegotten fiend! You don't have the power to keep me here forever!"

Asphodel laughed, and in the torchlight, his features appeared ghoulish. "Me? No, but Lucifer learned a valuable lesson when he created the Haven. He can create any number of places on Earth that negate angel powers. He's set up this little cave to administer physical punishment to misbehaving demons. He was hesitant to let any of the Host know about this locale, but I think we can agree the secret is safe with you." Asphodel pushed off the rock and took a step closer to me. "Also, I'm an incubus, not a fiend. But you knew that. What you may not know is that to anyone who matters, I am now the head incubus, and this little endeavor is going to make it official."

Incubus, fiend. Incubus, fiend. You know the difference. Fiends work for Beelzebub, Incubi work for Azrael. But Azrael is dead. Do I know the hierarchy of Hell anymore? Have I paid attention to anything in the past few years?

I shook my head, trying to shake off the insignificant details and focus on my predicament. I needed to calm down. I needed to count something. My gaze found the links in the chains attached to my wrists, and I let each round piece of metal become my world. *One, two, three, four, five, six, seven...* I continued on, until I counted eighteen links. *Eighteen is okay. Eighteen is divisible by three. Three is a sacred number. Three times... six. No. No. Not three sixes. Not three sixes.*

I flung my head to the side, only to see the eighteen links on my other wrist. I needed to think about how to get out of here. I needed to listen to Asphodel, though I was loath to take information from the self-proclaimed Prince of Lies.

"What do you want with me?" I meant to sound menacing, but my voice cracked, giving me the timbre of a scared teenage boy.

"I?" Asphodel placed a hand on his chest. "I want nothing. You're just a means to an end for me. I haven't seen a point in battling Heaven for some time now. Hell has clearly won the battle for the hearts and souls of Earth.

Because you're useless, I told myself. *Because you do nothing. Because you cannot even save* yourself *from the forces of Hell, much less all of humanity.*

An evil smile crept across Asphodel's face. "This is going to be so much fun." He didn't touch me, but he must have done something because before I could respond, the world fell away.

The war is over. I couldn't quite believe it, though I wasn't sure anymore what "it" signified. The idea of angels fighting angels was still unfathomable to me, despite the fact that the last few years had encompassed nothing else. I was battle-ready, yet sometimes I had prayed for one of Toriel's light blades to hit me and offer me a blessed twenty-four hours of oblivion, even if I knew Lucifer would gain the upper hand during my rest.

Lucifer. My brother and mentor had turned on God, and no matter how many times I stabbed him or begged him to surrender, he continued the rebellion. "God does not deserve our worship," he had said. "He makes us bow down before humans and serve them as his favored creations, when we are so much more than they are."

"It is not our place to decide our mission. We are made to serve, not question," I had replied.

Lucifer had laughed. "You forget I can see inside your head, Michael. All you do is question—me, yourself, God, everyone. You do not have what it takes to win this war or rule Heaven in my absence, and you know it. That is why I am going to win."

The self-doubt he knew was second nature to me had rushed in. I had rallied myself and blocked his next hit, but it didn't matter because after that, there was another and another and another. Eventually he'd retreated to plan his next offensive, for which I'd done my best to prepare. We'd repeated this pattern a hundred times during the war, and I hated the part of me that found the repetition comforting.

Finally one day, out of the blue, Lucifer had surrendered. He'd ordered his angels to lay down their arms, and all but one of them had obeyed. I had fallen on my knees and prayed to God for guidance. I'd expected no answer, as God so rarely responded to anything, and He had done nothing to quell Lucifer's rebellion. After only a moment, a flaming greatsword had appeared in front of me, and God had told me He would guide me in determining which angels should be struck through. I'd asked what would happen to those struck, but he'd remained silent. I'd resolved to trust his guidance.

I'd tested Gabriel first. I'd no doubt he would pass, and I needed my remaining loyal brother at my side as I performed this harrowing ordeal. Gabriel had stood on the spot God had set aside, a circle of blue flame on the ground that glowed in stark contrast to Heaven's gold. When no red sigil appeared above his head, I'd known I'd been right to trust him. Since then, I'd had a steady mark of cherubim standing in that same spot. Some had passed the test God had put to them, while others had demanded God's vengeance. The first time I'd passed my sword through a rebel, a lowly creature named Ysabel, she'd screamed as her body had turned to black smoke. Seemingly against her will—though who could tell the intentions of a cloud of smoke?—she'd been sucked through the portal to Earth.

Light take me. What have I done? I thought to myself. *Did I kill her? DId I destroy a fellow angel?* I'd glanced at Gabriel, and the horror on his face matched my inner turmoil. I'd known I'd have to stay strong to see this through, so none of my misgivings had shown on my face. "It is God's Will," I'd said to Gabriel, my voice harsher than I'd intended. Gabriel's queasy expression reminded me that I'd have to be strong for both of us.

After two weeks of judging cherubim—*letting God judge them,* I reminded myself—the time had come to judge the seraphim. I had almost inured myself to the terrifying sounds of smoke and suction that resulted every time I ran my sword through an opponent. None of the judgments had surprised me. The war had gone on for years, and we knew who the enemies were.

The first of the seraphim, though, was an uncertainty. Azrael had refused to fight in the war. She claimed the embodiment of love had no business fighting. I might have found her position sympathetic had she attempted to broker peace, but instead, she had spent most of her time on Earth, avoiding the conflict.

She was serving the people of Earth, as God intended. We have neglected our duties these past few years. Maybe she's right and we never should have fought. I took a deep breath and squared my shoulders. The decision was God's, not mine. I called out her name, and beautiful Azrael, with flowers in her dark red hair and a flowing white robe, stood before me. Her face remained calm, as if she trusted her God would not turn on her. I hoped she was right.

She stepped through the blue flames and held up her head to meet my gaze. I stared into the blue of her eyes before flicking my gaze up above her head. The red sigil I had come to dread shone there for only me to see. I hefted my sword.

"What? No!" Azrael held up her hands in what should have been a futile gesture to stop my blade, but I allowed her to say her piece. "I never joined Lucifer! I never fought! I've remained loyal to you!"

"Michael." Gabriel's voice held a plea even more desperate than Azrael's.

I closed my eyes for a moment, trembling uncertainty forming at the edge of my mind. I had an order from God, and if I were to defy it, I would be no better than those I condemned. "It is not my will, but God's." I swung my sword around and slashed it through her chest. Her screams echoed from where she'd stood long after the black smoke cleared, and I knew I would hear the remnants of that cry for years to come.

Against my will, I looked at Lucifer, and he had a small smile on his face, as if my—*God's*—condemnation of Azrael was a victory for him. I wished in that moment I had his gift so I could see into his mind. Was he pleased he had an extra angel on his side? Did he find pleasure in my performance of this small act of seeming evil? Did he simply enjoy watching angels suffer?

"Let us continue with this charade," said the next angel in line. Jophiel, angel of service, was nineteenth in the hierarchy, stepped into the flames. "Service to God, our higher angels, and even humanity is the only true calling, and I have always understood that."

"You defied me." Lucifer's voice was dry. "And I am clearly your better."

No red sigil appeared above Jophiel's head, as I had expected. He had been my right hand during this conflict, as he could stomach the battle better than Gabriel. I gave him a small nod, and he gave Lucifer a triumphant look before stepping out of the circle.

Next up was the Beast, Lucifer's loyal hound. I half expected to have to drag him into the flaming circle by the spiked collar he had taken to wearing once he joined the rebellion, but he walked into the flaming circle as the other's had. I hesitated only a moment when a red sigil appeared above his head. *He was being a good dog and obeying his master.* I shook my head. He may have chosen to stay in a dog's form, but he was as intelligent as any angel. He'd known what he was doing when he'd joined Lucifer's cause. I could not stay my blade.

I need a break, I thought. *I can't condemn my closest fellows like this.* I did not expect a respite, but somehow the world started spinning, and no further judgments came.

My head snapped back as I emerged back in Asphodel's cave, and my head smacked against the hard rock wall. I gritted my teeth and tried not to scream. I'd hit my head exactly where someone had bludgeoned me earlier.

I reoriented myself to my surroundings and reminded myself that the memories I couldn't quite shake were just that—memories. I didn't understand why they'd risen up so vividly, but I'd let them go millennia ago, or so I told myself.

Asphodel laughed. He remained where I'd left him, the eerie torchlight emphasizing his devilish features. "You've forgotten my power, haven't you, Michael?"

"Doesn't matter." My head pounded, but I mustered a glower for him. "Angel and demon powers don't work down here. You said so yourself."

"Michael, Michael, Michael. I told you this was my kingdom. It could hardly be that if I didn't have my powers. Lucifer has long desired to see you suffer, and I am just the demon to do it." He took a step closer. "I can't do what he can do. I can't read others' minds with barely a thought. But if I put some effort in, I can dig around in there. I can keep you living your wildest fantasies or worst nightmares in your own mind. It's not real, but you'll never know the difference. That's why I'm the Prince of Lies."

"Some prince. What I saw really happened."

"Yes, well, sometimes the truth is worse than the lies." That smug smile stayed glued to his face. "And as for that break you requested, I'm inclined to grant it for now. But Michael? We're just getting warmed up."

CHAPTER 5

Siren

GABRIEL TOOK HIS OWN SWEET time on his errand, whatever it was, and in the meantime, I braced myself for his inevitable reaction to the field angels. I thought about warning them he was coming, but in the interests of fairness, I figured they might as well be equally surprised. Besides, I didn't expect Gabriel to take so freaking long. So I spent more time than I wanted to pacing around the entrance to Heaven and glaring at anyone who walked by. I had a lot riding on these introductions, and I didn't like it. When Gabriel finally returned, he looked frazzled. He had just materialized in Heaven, but a number of strands of blond hair hung outside his ponytail. I could almost see circles under his eyes.

"We don't have to do this now if you're busy with something else." I meant to sound magnanimous, but my voice held its accustomed bite. Probably he thought I was being sarcastic. *Which maybe I am a bit.*

"No, no," said Gabriel. "Now is good. Did you arrange a meeting for the field angels?"

I laughed, and this time the bitterness in the sound was intentional. "They don't have meetings. They just... Well, it's probably better if you meet them one-on-one. Or one-on-two, I guess, since I'll be there."

"Won't that take awhile? Don't they have duties to attend to?'

I didn't need to have Lucifer's power to see the vision in Gabriel's head: a score of white-robed angels dispensing justice in response to the many prayers handed down from the prayer center. Despite my inability to lie, I didn't think he'd take me at my word if I told him he had no idea what he was in for. "Not so many as you might think" was all I said. Before he had time to ask what that meant, I grabbed his arm and led him toward Heaven's entrance. "I'll take you to the first one. You might want to wear something less respectable than you usually wear."

I pulled him down with me to Earth, and we materialized in a dark alley. Gabriel had replaced his usual blue button-down with a plaid one, and his khakis had lost their creases. "That's your idea of dressing down?" I asked. I had changed into a t-shirt and yoga pants, but then, I knew what was coming next.

Gabriel looked down at himself. "Isn't plaid casual?"

I stifled a laugh. "It's fine. It's not like you were going to blend in anyway." We rounded the corner to where two burly men stood outside a nondescript door. I'd always thought the club drew attention to itself by keeping its bouncers on the outside, but what did I know? I didn't recognize the man facing me, and I worried I might have a problem getting in, but then the other man turned around.

"Hey, Bill," I greeted him.

"Siren." Bill grinned at me. "You gonna give us a show tonight?"

"All signs point to yes," I said.

"You're the Siren?" said Bill's partner. "I've heard about you. I didn't think you'd be so... tiny."

"Good things come in small packages," said Bill. "Believe me, you don't want to mess with this one." I gave him a fierce grin as he eyed Gabriel. "Who's your friend?"

I inclined my head toward the archangel. "This is Gabriel. He won't give away your location." The bells in my head rang a discordant note, indicating my words might not be strictly true. I turned to Gabriel. "You want to go in here, right? Well, the rules say what happens in here stays in here."

He looked like he was going to ask more awkward questions, like where we were and why secrecy was so essential, but he glanced at Bill, swallowed, and nodded. "Fine. I won't tell anyone what I see."

I bared my teeth at Bill. "See? He's fine." The new bouncer looked dubious, but Bill opened the door and let us inside. I didn't think Bill believed Gabriel would stay quiet either—which was maddening. I hated it when people didn't believe me—but Bill also knew that his muscles didn't scare me.

The metal door clanked shut behind Gabriel and me as we walked down a short hallway into a dimly-lit room. We stepped into a mob of sweaty people whose cheers and jeers were focused on the large cage set on a pedestal in the room. Behind the wire, two men pummeled at each other, though the smaller one was clearly winning.

Gabriel squinted. "Is this a cage fight?" His tone suggested that could not possibly be what it was.

"Yup," I said. "Welcome to the underbelly of New York City."

"Why are we here? Are the field angels trying to shut this place down?" Gabriel's brow furrowed. "It's distasteful, but surely there are higher priorities."

I stared at Gabriel for a long moment and considered suggesting that we just leave. I wanted a job, but I wasn't sure it was worth the day I was about to have. *Too late to turn back now.* "Come on."

A bell rang, signifying the end of the fight. The larger of the fighters lay face-first on the mat inside the cage, and the more compact man wiped a trail of blood and sweat away from his nose and leaned outside the cage to grab a bottle of water from a nearby table. Enough people headed toward the window at the back of the room to collect their winnings that I could pull Gabriel up next to the cage. "We'd like a word with you," I said to the man inside.

The winner put down his water bottle and winked a crystal blue eye at me. "You know the rules, Lorelei."

"It's Siren," I said.

He smirked. "Same difference."

"Perhaps you didn't hear me." I pulled Gabriel up alongside me, cringing when he stumbled. "The *archangel* would like a word with you."

"I don't think you should tell him..." Gabriel trailed off as realization dawned on his face.

I gave them both a bitter smile. "Gabriel, meet Martyr, angel of sacrifice. Martyr, you already know Gabriel, your new boss."

Gabriel's mouth dropped open, but Martyr took the news in stride. "Lor, you know there's only one way to get me out of this cage. So are you coming up, or would the archangel like to go a round?"

The announcer was making noise about looking for a challenger, and hands of a few idiots went up around the room. The monetary reward for beating the champion was sizable, but these people should have known they didn't have a prayer against someone who looked like he'd fought for millennia. Before the bouncer could select one of the fools, I pulled myself up by the cage wires and swung around into the open door.

A few bouncers moved off the sides of the room, and the announcer looked about to say something, but they calmed down when they realized who had stepped into the cage. The announcer nodded at me and turned back to the crowd. "Looks like we've got a special treat for you tonight. The Siren vs. The Martyr! You have one minute to place your bets."

"You're getting weak," I said to Martyr as I bent over to touch my toes. I could teleport away any sore muscles I got from the fight, but I still warmed up on principle. "Did that guy actually give you a bloody nose?"

"I have to let them hit me sometimes." He leaned against the cage wall, watching me with a small smile on his face. "Otherwise it's hardly sporting." When I snorted, he shook his head. "Not everyone hates humans like you do, Lor."

"Touché, though that's not what I meant. Sporting is not a good word to describe these fights on the best of days, and you're hardly a fair fight."

"True, though it's for a good cause." He watched me for a moment. "What does the archangel want?"

I jogged in place. "I told you. He's your new boss. He asked to lead the field angels, and Michael agreed."

The smirk fell away from Martyr's face for the first time since he'd seen me. "Does he know how things stand?"

"I'm introducing him slowly." I twisted to stretch my torso. "Are you seriously having a conversation with me before I beat you?"

The smile returned. "So confident."

"Well, you seem curious about what Gabriel wants, so I figure that gives me an edge."

"You always think you have an edge."

"Because I always do."

"I hope your bets are placed!" called out the announcer as Martyr and I stepped into place. "Because the fight will begin in three... two... one..." A bell rang.

Martyr and I dropped into fighting stances, legs apart as we balanced on the balls of our feet. For an entire minute, we stared at each other, and I'm sure from the audience, we seemed to do nothing. In actuality, we knew each other's tells so well that each fight played out in our heads before we could move. I prepared a punch, but the slight tilt of his head told me he saw it coming. He shifted to kick, then saw me alter my stance to block.

The audience rumbled, beginning to get restless. They had paid to see a fight after all, not watch Martyr and I stand still as statues. Around the time I heard the first boo, I threw a punch I knew Martyr would block.

"So impatient." Martyr's mocking held more amusement than malice.

"Someone has to be," I said as I ducked under his roundhouse kick. I tried to spin around in time to set him off balance, but he was as fast as I was. "Though that does raise the question. If you got kicked out of the cage for taking too long, would you have a conversation with me?"

"We'll never know, will we?" he asked as we blocked a rapid flurry of each other's blows, then sprung apart, our breathing only slightly heavier than usual. "For someone who claims not to care what humans think, you react awfully quickly to their poor opinion."

"I didn't punch you—"

"Try to punch me."

"—because of the crowd. I just want to get this ridiculous charade over with."

We watched each other for only a few more seconds before Martyr attempted to bull rush me. I jumped up to grab the wire roof of the cage and swung my legs up to evade him. "Now who's impatient?" I asked, twisting my legs around his neck, hoping but not really expecting to immobilize him.

"Hey, gotta put on a show for the crowd. This is my full-time job." With brute strength that would always surpass mine, he yanked on my legs, forcing me to give up my hold on the bars. I rolled off his shoulders and bounced back to my feet.

The fight continued in this manner for some time, our tactics evenly matched. The crowd loved every minute of it, or at least I assumed so. I only barely registered the cheering, and I was making a point not to look at Gabriel.

I could imagine the horrified look on his face, and I knew seeing it in person would only distract me.

Eventually, I decided it was time to end the fight, partly because I was tired and partly because I was worried Gabriel hadn't stuck around to see the outcome. Martyr had to be more tired than I was. He'd been fighting all evening, after all, though he was more accustomed to long bouts than I was.

Martyr had said earlier I always thought I had an edge, and he was right. He might—only might—have been a better fighter than me, but he would always give up before I did. He spent day and night winning cage fights around the world, but secretly, he wanted to lose. He was the angel of sacrifice. Taking hits was in his nature.

When I got tired enough of our back and forth, I increased my speed, delivering an onslaught of kicks and punches that he had no trouble blocking. But this time, when he tried to step away, I didn't let him. I continued my assault, peppering him with every strike in my arsenal.

"End game, is it, Lor?" He reached out to grab me by the neck, and as I lifted both arms between his to cast them aside, he crooked a foot behind my knee and yanked, knocking me to the floor. At the last moment, I dropped into a crouch and spun my other leg around to trip him as well. He landed with a thud on his chest, and before he could push himself up, I knelt on his back and twisted one of his arms against his back.

He cringed. "You know I could get out of this, right?"

"I do." After all, he had a hand and two legs free. "I also know we could be at this all day, and eventually Gabriel will leave. You don't want that, do you?"

He twisted his head up just enough to give me a glance that said I knew him too well. Then he held up his free hand in a gesture of surrender. The bell rang, and the announcer made some noise about me being the winner. I let go of Martyr, then offered him a hand to help him up, which he took. He gestured at the cage door and said, "Ladies first." When I glowered at him, he smirked and headed toward the entry before me. I followed, but before I could cross the threshold, a hand on my arm stopped me.

"You know the rules," the announcer said to me. "You're the champ now, which means you have to fight challengers until you lose."

I put nine thousand years of built-up disdain into my glare. "Do we have to? You know how this is going to end."

He had the decency to cower a bit, but he stood his ground. "Get back in the cage, and maybe put a little effort in this time."

I looked down on him for a moment longer. I could leave. This greasy, pathetic human couldn't keep me here, but if I left, it would make Martyr's life more difficult. I stomped back into the cage and made my way to the side where Gabriel stood, his face looking pretty much as I expected. I looked around for Martyr and found him heading back toward the ticket counter. He always bet on himself, and even with his most recent loss, he probably had a truckload of winnings to collect.

"Give me a minute," I said to Gabriel over the voice of the announcer calling for a challenger. "I've got to let some guy pummel me before I can finish our introductions."

"Siren, what is going on?" I could barely hear Gabriel's hiss over the thrum of the crowd. "Why is a field angel the champion of a cage fighting ring?"

I didn't want to explain, but I was going to have to figure out how. The questions were going to keep coming as the introductions continued, and I'd known that when I volunteered to do this. "He's the angel of sacrifice. It's in his nature to take hits for the greater good."

Gabriel's voice got higher and louder. "How is this for the greater good? I seriously doubt the prayer center has sent down orders to behave like a common thug!"

"The thing about the prayer center is—" Before I could explain, a large hand grabbed my upper arm. I turned to see a tall man in a muscle shirt with several days worth of stubble on his chin and a tattoo of a snake on his arm.

"You gonna fight, or you gonna talk to pretty boy over there?" His tone suggested I should be afraid of him.

I wasn't. "I mean, which would you rather do?"

His head jerked backwards. "Fight, of course!"

I stood up and stretched my arms. "Honestly? Me too. But we all do what we must. I take it that it's time to get this party started."

He growled. "I am going to pound you into the ground, little girl."

I arched an eyebrow at him but said nothing. I couldn't lie, after all. The bell rang, and the growler didn't even try to take my measure before throwing a punch in my face. It wasn't a bad hit, but it had nothing on the smacks I had taken from Martyr. Nonetheless, I let the impact of the fighter's fist roll through me and knock me into the cage. I slumped to the ground and held up my hand in surrender.

The growler looked confused, and I hoped he wasn't the type to keep going until the bouncers pulled him off me. After a moment, he held up his hands in victory. Before the bell rang, I hopped up and ducked out of the cage. The announcer grabbed my arm again. "Seriously, Siren, was that the best you could do?"

"Nope! But it's the best I'm giving you."

"You're killing me, baby," he said. "Now I'm stuck with this idiot as champion until Martyr steps back into the cage."

"I'd say I'm sorry for your profits, but we'd both know it was a lie."

"Anytime you want to come back, you just say the word. This could be a full-time gig for you. Just think, I'd have two champions!"

I gave him a broad smile. "You disgust me." I hopped down from the platform and went to meet Gabriel and Martyr around the side.

"—should be attending to the prayers of humanity, not fighting in some disgusting cage." Gabriel sounded angry, which surprised me. He and Martyr were two of the most easy-going angels I knew.

Martyr glanced my way as I came around the corner. He had that same small, smug smile on his face, but it was a little strained. "Hey, Lor. The archangel here was just reprimanding me for my life choices. Care to join him?"

I had more than once suggested that Martyr do something with his immortality other than suffer repeated traumatic brain injuries, but I went over to stand next to him rather than Gabriel. I didn't approve of Martyr's cage fighting because I was pretty sure it was a reflection of his own self-loathing. The archangel had no idea why the field angels made the choices they did, and to come in with harsh words blazing was unfair. I was about to rip him a new one when I remembered I really wanted a Heavenly job, and only Gabriel would consider giving me one.

Looks like I'm playing mediator, which is a role that should never fall to me. "Gabriel," I said with all the patience I could muster. "I know you find Martyr's choice of occupation surprising, but I think if you listened to him—"

Gabriel pointed at Martyr. "He's already admitted he doesn't listen to requests from the prayer center. He chooses to spend his days in this hole instead. What more could I possibly need to know?"

I felt a headache coming on that had nothing to do with the punch to the face I'd just taken. I'd decided to introduce Martyr to Gabriel first because he was the easiest field angel to get along with, but I hadn't taken into account his taciturn nature. I was also out of patience. "Is that really the most helpful thing you could have said?"

Martyr arched an eyebrow at me but didn't seem offended. "I work with what I'm given, Lor."

Gabriel stood up straighter, and his facial expression looked as if he'd stolen it from Michael. "Martyr, I will give you one last chance. Will you join a team of field angels under my direction and obey the tenets Heaven sets forth?"

Martyr's smirk didn't waver. "Not on your life."

"Then I don't have anything further to say to you," said Gabriel.

Martyr let out a bitter laugh. "We never had anything to say." He turned to me, and his smile turned a bit more sincere. "You going to see Jubiel next?"

If I don't abandon this whole ridiculous endeavor. I nodded.

"Great. I've got a package for him." He hefted a heavy duffle back from the ground next to him and handed it to me. "You're welcome back any time, Lor The archangel?." He looked Gabriel up and down. "Well, we'll see."

Martyr walked around to the front of the cage, where the announcer was once more looking for competitors. "I challenge!"

Gabriel's nose was wrinkled in disgust. It wasn't a good look for him. "Tell me that was the worst of them."

"Oh, Gabriel." I grabbed his hand as I reached out with my angel senses to find where Jubiel was hiding out these days. "You know I can't lie."

CHAPTER 6

Bedlam

I PULLED UP OUTSIDE KHET'S APARTMENT in my shiny new red BMW convertible. I honked the horn to let her know I was there and snapped my fingers a few times to the beat, ready to put my plan into action.

Wait, you have a plan? That's a first.

Well, strictly speaking, it's not so much a plan as an idea. Do you think I need a plan?

When have you ever planned anything?

The woman whom I was absolutely, definitely going to fall in love with at some point in the very near future emerged from her apartment wearing a sweater and jeans much better suited to a road trip than a romantic interlude. I supposed since I had invited her on a road trip and not a romantic interlude, her attire was appropriate. Perhaps it was even auspicious, as it meant the mind reader hadn't yet uncovered my plot.

She turned around after locking up the apartment and put her hands on her hips. "Did you seriously buy a convertible in the middle of December? I hope you don't expect me to ride around with the top down."

"Umm..." I hadn't really thought that one through. I had envisioned an exciting convertible road trip with our hair blowing in the wind, but I supposed it was a little cold for that, even for me.

She shook her head, seeming bemused. "Pop the trunk for me, would you?" She lifted up a black and red suitcase. "Some of us can't materialize clothes out of thin air and need to pack."

I pressed the little trunk button on the extra key fob, and the car beeped and flashed its lights. "Should be open."

"I don't really mind about the convertible," said Khet as she put her suitcase in the trunk. "Just so long as you keep it. Maybe we can go on a summer road trip."

Hm. She seems perfectly friendly and normal and not in love with me at all. Maybe I do need a plan.

Maybe she's secretly been in love with me for years and didn't say anything because of the whole Keziel situation.

She's had three months to do something about that.

Yeah, but she's been with Gabriel. The timing's been bad.

Somehow I don't think—

The passenger car door slammed, pulling me out of my inner dialogue. Khet sat beside me, fastening her seatbelt. "You should fasten yours, too."

"You do realize I can't die, right?" I pulled the uncomfortable strap around me. "I can't even get injured for long."

"It's the law, Bedlam. Speaking of, you didn't answer my question." She looked at me expectantly.

Shit. I didn't hear a question.

So ask her to repeat it.

But then I might have to admit why I wasn't paying attention.

"Oh, sorry," I said. "Yes, absolutely."

She relaxed. "Sorry to make you go to Pennsylvania, not that it's a big deal for you, I guess. I really need to get a guy around here."

Wait, what? I didn't go to Pennsylvania. Why would I go to Pennsylvania? And what does she mean she needs a guy around here? I'm her guy around here.

Maybe you should fess up to lying.

Nah, that might encourage her to get another guy. I'm sure it'll be fine.

I pressed the button to put the top up on the car, then turned the volume up on the speakers. I wanted loud music so Khet wouldn't be able to hear my thoughts, so I went with Megadeth. I put the car into gear and took off down the street. Before I had gotten halfway down the street, Khet had reached out to change the radio station. When "Sweating Bullets" continued to pound out of the speakers no matter how many times she pressed "scan," she slumped back in her seat. "What's with the death metal?"

"Khet, I am disappointed in you. This is clearly thrash metal." I snapped my fingers, and the speakers blared out "Chainsaw Lust" by Necrophagia. "*This* is death metal."

She rubbed her temples. "Whatever it is, can we please listen to something quieter? Or nothing at all? I still want to know more about this angelic mission we're going on."

I pressed the button on the steering wheel that lowered the volume but left the metal on. "I told you. I was sworn to secrecy."

"Since when do you keep secrets?'

Since I realized if I tell you what's really going on, you'll yell at me to stop this road trip nonsense?

That's great. You want a relationship, and you're lying to her. Aren't you always on her case for hiding the truth from Gabriel?

That's different.

I turned to her, my eyes as wide and innocent as I could make them. "Do you really want me to violate Heaven's trust when they've finally put some in me again?"

She pointed her finger at the windshield to indicate I should look at the road. "Somehow I suspect you've already violated Heaven's trust by involving me."

She knows me too well.

That's why we're perfect for each other.

If you say so.

"If you won't tell me what we're doing, will you at least tell me where we're going?" Khet pulled a fold-up map of the United States out of her purse. "That way at least I can navigate."

"Seriously, Khet? A giant map? What is this, 1985? We have got to get you a cell phone."

"I'm still working on the laptop. Let's take things one step at a time." Khet unfolded the map and twisted it around until it presumably showed Maryland. "So are you telling me where we're going or not?"

I reached out with my mind to locate Lethe. "We're heading to Los Angeles for now, though I suppose that could change. I don't need you to navigate for me, though. We can just take I-70 to Utah, then pick up I-15 to LA."

Khet frowned at her map. "I don't think that's the fastest route out of Maryland. It looks like we'd be better off if we took I-68. Besides, I-70 merges with the Pennsylvania turnpike for a while, and the tolls there are crazy."

Douchebag's flaming sword, we're arguing about directions! Like a real couple! My plan is working!

Isn't arguing about directions usually a later-in-the-relationship thing?

I waved my hand to dismiss either her words or my thoughts. "You don't care about tolls. Besides, if we go up through Pennsylvania, we'll be closer to the Archives of the Afterlife."

"The what now?"

"It's a museum in West Virginia that's got all kinds of creepy, demon-possessed artifacts."

Khet peered at me. "Can demons possess artifacts? I know it doesn't go so well when they possess humans."

"Of course they can't," I said. "But people think they do, and it's great. See, coincidence happens, but people never believe that. They'll chalk it up to a series of sixes they found. Occasionally a demon will latch onto that paranoia and feed it by causing accidents and whatnot." I knew what Khet was going to say. "Demons. Not me. At least, not in a very long time. The cursed object game is a very tired trope. Besides, you've set me on the straight and narrow."

Khet snorted. "You may be an angel now, but no one would describe your path as 'straight and narrow.'"

"Thank God for that. Homophobic language aside, straight and narrow sounds boring."

We drove for several hours in a mix of idle conversation and companionable silence. Khet talked about what she had learned in her classes that semester, and I did my best to pay attention. I told her about the television shows I had been watching, but I don't think she appreciated all the jokes. I eventually turned the music to something more her speed, and we belted out the entire Wicked soundtrack along with Idina Menzel and Kristen Chenoweth.

After about five hours on the road, we arrived in Moundsville, West Virginia, home of the Archives of the Afterlife. When we walked in the door to the Sanford Center, a man greeted us. "Are you here for the Zumba class?"

"Nope!" I said. "We want to see the creepy crawlies upstairs."

He shuddered. "I certainly hope they haven't been crawling around. Better you than me going up there. I've never seen so many unsettling dolls in my life."

Khet paled. "Dolls?"

I laughed. "Don't tell me you're scared of dolls." I started toward the stairs.

Khet waved her farewell to the Zumba instructor and headed after me. "Have you known me to own a doll? Ever?"

"Come to think of it, no." I grinned. "But you know what I am now getting you every Christmas for the rest of your natural life?"

Khet shuddered. "Then it's a good thing my natural life was over a long time ago."

We entered the archive and paid our $5 admission—the couples rate, I was excited to see. The guy downstairs had been right. The tiny museum hosted a lot of creepy dolls, most of them porcelain with big black eyes, but other artifacts graced the shelves as well, and each of them had a little placard explaining its supernatural history and properties.

"Hey, look, Khet!" I pulled her over to a doll that bore a striking resemblance to *The Exorcist* baby. "This one says it sometimes gives off comforting vibes. Maybe it's angel-blessed."

Khet glared at me. "No. No, it is not. Also, I have met enough angels to know they would not spend their time blessing dolls."

I bounced on my toes. "Aw, come on. You need to get into the spirit of things." I read a few more placards, hoping I might find something to interest her. Most of the items said things like, "I found this in an antique shop, and it called to me," but a few had more persuasive histories.

"Check out this Bible! A guy found it open to page 666 with an angel statue on top of it. He removed the statue and took it home, and then his cat died."

"Was his cat sick?"

"Probably." My shoulder slumped, but I dragged her over to a colorful Doctor Seuss book with a stain on the cover. "How about this children's book? Weird things started happening after a family bought it at a garage sale, and they discovered it had previously belonged to a child who had died in a quadruple homicide."

Khet gave the book a sympathetic look. "That's so sad." She looked pensive for a moment, and I thought she might be reflecting on her own dead child. "You know, I don't know a lot about what happens to people after they die. I mean, I've heard the screams of the damned, so I guess I know what happens to some people. But do humans ever die and become ghosts?"

"Nope!"

Hm. That came out more cheerful than I intended.

I think it's reasonable to be grateful for a lack of ghosts.

"I guess that makes sense. I can't imagine that Lucifer would let one of his souls go, and from what I hear of Uriel, he's equally possessive." Khet glanced at a broken doll with a wire dress frame and shuddered. "Can we go now? Haunted or no, this place gives me the willies."

"Are you sure? I think they do overnight stays. You could separate your soul from your body and try to communicate with the haunted objects."

Khet glared at me. "I hate you."

I'd have been worried if I thought she meant it. "No, you don't."

"No, I don't, but I'm still leaving." She headed back toward the stairs.

I rushed to catch up to her. "I thought we'd stop for the night in Columbus. There's this great Chinese place on High Street. Maybe tomorrow the Model T Ford Museum in Indiana?"

"So long as there are no creepy dolls, that sounds good to me."

CHAPTER 7

Michael

ASPHODEL SAID I COULD HAVE a break, and part of me wanted to try to sleep and recover what sanity I could before he played whatever sick game next occurred to him. I was of the school of thought, though, that the first duty of a prisoner was to escape. If Lucifer wanted me trapped here, I wanted the opposite on principle. Besides, with Asphodel gone, the cave was pitch black, and loath as I was to admit it, I was afraid of the dark.

I need to be smart about this. All my instincts screamed for me to struggle against my chains like a madman, but brute force would not help me. I needed to quell my fears and think my way out of these chains. *The chains are bolted to the wall. If I try hard enough, perhaps I can unscrew them.* I twisted my arm around to reach the bolts with more ease than I expected, but my large fingers had a difficult time grasping the almost-flat bolts. I dug at them with my fingernails and used all the might of my muscular form to try to get the connector to budge. For hours I tried, through what might have been night or day, and the only results were blisters on my thumb and grime underneath my ragged fingernails.

You're useless. You're going to be stuck here forever. You deserve it. No one will miss you because you don't do anything good or useful anyway.

Deep breaths. Deep breaths. I needed to quiet the self-doubt. I counted to seven over and over again. I shouted the numbers into the vast void that surrounded me, but my mind kept coming back to the triple sixes of the chains that bound me.

Think, Michael. Think. You can figure a way out of this. I couldn't. Thinking had never been my strong suit, since most of the time my thoughts were a jumbled mess I wanted to escape from. The only thing I was good at was striking down demons with the fury of my sword. Maybe I was a fool for trying to think of any solution other than pulling the chains out of their sockets.

I jerked at the chains, hoping a hard, fast yank would do the trick. When it didn't, I tried again, hoping the first effort—or first five efforts—had loosened the stone around the iron. I then tried a longer, more sustained effort. I pushed my whole body forward, hoping some weakness in the chains would give way. When my arms seeped blood from where the chains cut into me, I gave up. *No escape. No escape. No escape.*

I screamed with a primal rage and thrashed against the wall and chains. I banged my head, my feet, and my back against the hard, rough surface, and I didn't care. Asphodel thought he had given me a break from the torture, but I would never find release from the misery of my own failure.

Cain. I need Cain. She's the only one who can make the voices stop. My runaway thoughts were the least of my problems, but I couldn't escape the sheer yearning for the only person in millennia who had brought me relief. *She'll never come for me. She doesn't know I'm here. She can't find me. And if she could, would she even come? I'm stuck here, and I'll never see her again.*

After a time I could not measure, I had worn myself out. Every part of me hurt, and I wanted nothing more than blissful unconsciousness. I considered smashing my head against the wall with enough force to knock myself out, but I thought better of it. I didn't know what would happen to me if I died down here. Without my angel powers, I might die permanently.

Wouldn't that be a relief? I'd be free of my responsibilities. Someone else could take over. Someone less useless. A tear came to my eye. *Thank the Lord no one is here to see me cry.* I could always keep my cool. I prided myself on that, but I couldn't hold myself together when the situation was so hopeless and no one was there to see me fall apart. I needed to get it out of my system before Asphodel returned. I leaned back against the wall and tried to think of it as a strong, cool, steady support instead of a prison. Eventually it must have worked, because I fell into a fitful doze.

No rest for the wicked. The words popped into my head before I could stop them. I wasn't wicked. I was doing the Lord's will, condemning the seraphim who had betrayed Him. I counted upward and concluded that the next angels would be safe. Sybil and Somniel were trusted advisors, despite their taciturn natures. They had taken on the responsibility of watching Siren after the unfortunate incident with the Grigori, and I had no reason to question their loyalty.

Should you question Siren's loyalty? She remained true to her angel calling when the rest of the Grigori did not. She sounded the alarm that started the war. She cannot lie. Why do you doubt her?

I snapped my head up, pushing off the irrelevant thoughts. "Somniel," I said, my voice a harsh bark. I swung my sword around and pointed it at the middle of the blue flames. She stepped forward, and the Lord cleared her. Sybil, too, passed muster. I was about to call on Raphael, who didn't have a deceitful shard in his soul, when the angel Toriel entered the room. "Michael! We've caught him!"

I stopped myself before my sigh of relief became audible. Lucifer should have given us the most trouble of the rebels, as he was the most powerful. One lowly cherub, though, had used guerilla tactics against us and given us more trouble than the rest of Lucifer's cadre combined. He had also refused to surrender with Lucifer and had been wreaking havoc on Earth in all the days since. "Show him in."

Toriel's friend Raquel entered, holding a light blade to the throat of a feral angel. The rebel struggled against Raquel's grasp, but he couldn't use the full force of his strength without risking injury from the sword at his jugular.

"Bedlam." I had not known I could put such venom into a single word until that moment. "Put him in the circle." Raquel shoved Bedlam forward, but the nimble angel sidestepped him and broke free of his captor's grasp. A collective gasp went up around the room, as the gathered crowd realized their only remaining enemy was free and in their midst.

Bedlam did not attack. He gave me the darkest look I had ever seen on an angel's face. "You think you can condemn me? You?" He snarled. "You aren't worthy to breathe my air!"

Keziel stepped forward, a pained expression on her face. She was the only weapon in our arsenal against Bedlam, and had she been judged, she would have been the one out searching for him, as she well knew. "Bedlam, please!"

Bedlam turned his head to face her, the motion more like that of an animal than a man. He stared at her, expressionless, and I thought for a moment he might step into the circle and face judgment as the Lord intended. Instead, he roared and hurtled toward me. I braced myself for a fight, but to my surprise, instead of launching himself at me, he threw himself onto the judgment sword. As the flaming blade pierced his torso, his scream turned into maniacal laughter that faded to nothing as his body turned to smoke.

Keziel's horrified gasp broke the silence, though Jophiel snatched her arm and pulled her back into place beside him. "It's as it should be," he said.

A tiny tickle at the back of my head wondered if that was true. The Lord was meant to carry out all judgments against the angels, but Bedlam had judged himself. *That proves he was even more guilty. Thinking himself above the Lord.* Still part of me realized I would never know whether the Lord had condemned Bedlam. *Of course he would have. He would have, but he didn't.* The nagging uncertainty would eat at me all my days.

I didn't know if the pounding in my head or the faint sound of someone approaching roused me from my dream, but as the fog cleared from my head, I became aware I would soon have company. The tiniest bit of light emerged from where I had seen a tunnel to my right, and the luminescence grew as the light footsteps grew louder. *Asphodel, come to renew his torments,* I thought, but the sounds were too delicate, barely a brush against stone. A wobbling lantern came into view, spreading beams of light through the cave, and behind it, a tiny woman's figure. I couldn't make out her features, but if I didn't need to. I knew her white-blond hair and coal-dark eyes better than my own face in the mirror. *My Lethe.*

I cringed at my immediate association with the archdemon. I did not want to love someone whose wails had driven countless humans to suicide, but my traitorous heart called out to her anyway. I had not seen Lethe often in the millennia since I'd cast her into the Abyss. At first she had dogged my footsteps every time I went to Earth.

She wanted redemption and thought I could offer it. I could have explained to her that the Lord judged her, not I, but instead I had turned a cold shoulder to her pleas. Eventually, she stopped asking.

What kind of angel abandons the woman he loves? You could have helped her find her way back to you. I told myself I hadn't known the Lord would ever welcome a demon back into his embrace, and that was true enough. Until Bedlam rose from the dead, none of the damned had earned redemption. The reality, though, was that I hadn't helped her because her betrayal had cut too deep, and I could not forgive it. She had fallen apart over the millennia, losing her mind as surely as she had lost whatever was left of her virtue. Even in the dim light, I could tell that her hair hung ragged, and if I looked hard enough, I could see the circles underneath her eyes.

"Come to join in Asphodel's games?" My voice rasped, worn out from all the screaming I had done before I had slept.

Lethe rushed forward, holding the lantern up to my face. "Oh, my Michael! What have they done to you?"

I turned my head away from the sudden bright light and remained silent. How could I tell her that "they" had done nothing to me, because I had done most of the damage to myself? Besides, the wounds were obvious. *Are they? Are my wounds ever obvious, or do I spend so much time hiding the ones deep inside? I am trapped in Asphodel's prison, and that is far worse than any cut or bruise.*

Lethe put down her lantern and pulled an iron key out of the pocket of her dress. She put a gentle hand on my arm and lifted it closer to her, then unlocked the cuff on my wrist. As the shackle fell away, the pale white skin where it had hung stood out in stark contrast to the rest of my blood-speckled arm.

"What are you doing?" I asked.

"Oh, Michael, I heard you were imprisoned down here." Her high-pitched voice filled with anguish as it echoed through the cavern. "I couldn't bear it! I had to rescue you!"

She was still holding onto my wrist, and I turned my hand around to clutch her arm instead. "Where did you get the key? Did you steal it from Lucifer? I'm here under his orders. If you defy him, I don't know what he'll do to you."

I shouldn't care. She's a wretched demon. Visions of what Lucifer did to demons who disobeyed him swam through my mind. I could still remember when Lucifer stabbed Azrael through with the Spear of Destiny, but I imagined Lethe's crumpled form on that beach. I envisioned her chained next to me, forced to suffer whatever torments I did. I didn't know if I could continue under such circumstances.

"I don't care what Lucifer thinks." Lethe unlocked my other cuff. "I no longer follow him. If Bedlam can gain redemption, then anyone can, even me. I am traveling the Earth doing good, and one day, I'll return to you."

She'll return to me. The idea should have filled me with joy, but instead all I felt was a bitter resignation. The angel in me could never stop loving her, and it wanted her by my side again. Another part of me, though until this moment I never would have thought I had an unangelic part, knew I could never trust her again. *And she feels that I betrayed her. We could never make each other happy. Light, though, do I want to be miserable with her again.* I hated that I wanted that, and I wished there were a way to free myself from my love.

I rubbed my arms. *I should stay and insist she go.* But I wasn't that unselfish. "Do you know the way out of here?"

A look of devastation crossed Lethe's face, and I wondered if she hated how easily I had let her sacrifice herself. "I don't think you'll make it out in your condition. It's a long walk."

"I can handle it." My words sounded strong and determined even as I doubted them. I could barely stand, and the rocks dug into my bare feet. "I can handle anything."

"Oh, my Michael. So brave." She reached out, as if she planned to touch my face but then thought better of it. "I have a better idea. I'll take you to my corner of this little cavern, where you can rest and recover until you're ready to leave."

"If I can just get out of here, I can teleport myself to safety and health." *Physical health, at any rate.* "Please, just show me the way out."

"Are you sure?" She held the lantern up to my face and studied me. Something she saw must have convinced her, because she nodded. "Very well. Follow me."

As I followed her out of the cave, I asked, "What did you mean, your corner of this cavern?"

She didn't glance back at me as she answered, and I couldn't help but feel that was intentional. "This complex stretches for miles. Lucifer thought it would be useful if each of his archdemons had a place on Earth where only their powers worked." She drew in a ragged breath. "I never used it to torture angels, I swear."

"Who did you torture then?" Judgment laced my tone. "Demons? Humans?"

"You don't know how hard it's been." I could hear the tears in her voice. "You don't know what it's like to be condemned to Hell. Down there, it's all dark and nothingness. I had to use all my power to carve a stronghold for myself, and even then, other demons were always trying to take my place. It's not like Heaven, where everyone wants to serve. Demons want power, and sometimes I needed to put my banshees back in line." My lip curled as she talked about torture like it was a reasonable option. "But all that is over now. I'm going to be good. I'm going to earn my way back into Heaven."

We came to an intersection in the caves, and Lethe looked down each hallway, as if considering her options. "Don't you know the way out?" I asked.

"Of course I do!" Her head snapped around to look at me, and her demonic eyes glinted before her expression softened. "I'm just trying to figure out which way is fastest." She inclined her head toward the passage to the right. "This way, I think."

I followed where she led, realizing I was entirely at her mercy. The caverns held no light except the lantern she carried, and the place seemed to be a maze. I followed her down a long, narrow passageway. Though tiny Lethe moved with grace through the corridor, I had to duck a few times where the ceiling was low and turn sideways once to get through a particularly tight part. Eventually the hallway opened up into a larger cavern, and I breathed a sigh of relief as I stepped into the open air. Then I realized the cavern was a dead end.

I turned to Lethe. "What—?"

She pulled on a lever sticking out of the wall, and an iron portcullis rattled down behind me. I moved to dive under it before it fell, but in my weakened state, I lacked the maneuverability. I turned back to Lethe, the question no doubt apparently on my face.

She gave me an evil smile. "Welcome to my corner of this dungeon. You're my prisoner now."

CHAPTER 8

Siren

GABRIEL AND I APPEARED IN a hidden spot a few blocks away from Trafalgar Square. I noticed in the dim light of the dusty alley that Gabriel had changed back into his accustomed blue shirt and khaki pants. He gave our surroundings a questioning look, and had to resist rolling my eyes. *Does he just appear in the middle of crowds?*

"You didn't have to be such an asshole to Martyr," I said as I led us out into the main streets. The light didn't get much brighter in the open air, given the cloudy skies, but the wind picked up a fair bit. "Believe it or not, he's one of the good guys."

Gabriel kept pace beside me, seemingly unaffected by the chill in the air. "He flat-out refused to do his duty. He participates in illegal cage fights and refuses to talk to anyone who won't fight him. How could he possibly be 'one of the good guys'?" I opened my mouth to answer, but Gabriel held up a hand. "I know, I know. You can't lie. I believe you think he's one of the good guys, but your opinion is suspect."

I took a deep breath and reminded myself to be patient. "You don't have to be an asshole to me, either. I'm just doing what you asked, and I told you you weren't going to like it."

Gabriel sighed. "Just... introduce me to the next field angel, please."

"What did you think I was doing?"

For some reason, that made Gabriel smile. "Now who's the asshole?"

"It's in character for me." I slung Martyr's bag further up on my shoulder and strode faster.

Despite the weather, Trafalgar Square was full of tourists and buskers. I made my way past a woman with a guitar singing about her lost love and a guy with the ugliest yellow hair I had ever seen snapping pictures of her. I pushed past a line of tourists feeding pigeons and approached a seated man with dark skin and dreadlocks wearing, of all things, a light t-shirt that said "What Would I Do?"

"Step right up, step right up!" the man called out in a Cockney accent. He spun three upside-down cups on the small table in front of him at a dizzying pace. "Find the bean, double your money! Step right up!"

I did as I was bidden and sat down across from him.

"Give us a smile, love," he said, his own smile distant, until he focused on my face. He dropped both the grin and the fake accent and said in a flat, American dialect, "Oh, it's you."

"It's me!" I said with false cheer. "And believe me, you don't want me guessing where the bean is. Though I suppose I wouldn't mind you doubling my money." I patted the duffel bag.

"Been to see Martyr then, have you?" The runner of the shell game, also known as Jubiel, reached out to take the bag from me. "I'll see that gets where it needs to go. Was that all you wanted?"

I gave a humorless laugh. "Nope. I'm here to introduce you to your new boss." I gestured for Gabriel to step forward. Gabriel, for his part, looked slightly less shocked than he had at the cage fights, but I expected this encounter to go downhill quickly.

Jubiel looked Gabriel up and down. "That's the archangel Gabriel." He didn't sound impressed.

"Yes, yes, it is," I said. "He petitioned Michael for leadership of the field angels, and I'm introducing him to you guys."

Jubiel snorted. "What are they paying you to do that?"

"I get to join the team."

Jubiel rocketed to his feet, knocking over his table. "You think you can join the field angels because Michael and Gabriel say so? You know that's not how we work!"

I jumped up as well, though internally I remained calm. Jubiel didn't take change well, and he responded by lashing out at the instigator of said change. I knew if I called him on his bullshit and was confrontational right back, he'd back down.

Gabriel didn't know that, though, and his response was measured and disdainful. "How do you work then? By being a petty con artist in service to the Lord?"

Jubiel's nostrils flared. "Better than abandoning my duty for two thousand years to chase after some human girl."

Gabriel's face reddened, his temper heating up to match Jubiel's. "I have always done the Lord's work. I have spent the last two thousand years performing acts of charity. I did a lot more for humanity then than I've done since returning to Heaven, that's for sure."

"Well, then, run away again, archangel. No one wants you here." Jubiel leaned forward and straightened his table.

He had calmed down. I should have been grateful for that, but my contrarily honest nature took over. "Giving someone a hard time for running away? That's rich coming from you."

"Hey." Jubiel pointed a finger at me, though his voice held considerably less malice than when he had spoken to Gabriel. "You know very well why I am off the radar, and it's all for the cause of good."

Gabriel perked up at that. "Really? Why?" Ever the optimist, he no doubt envisioned Jubiel running honest shell games in order to survive after some dire misfortune.

Jubiel grinned and lowered his voice. "I got a job with a multi-billion dollar finance corporation, then embezzled millions from them."

"What?" Gabriel's voice came out as a squeak. "How is that the cause of good?"

Jubiel spread his arms wide. "Hey, hey. I'm the angel of charity. Of course I donated it. Rob from the rich and give to the poor and all that. Those fat cats at the finance companies make money hand over fist and pay pennies out to both their customers and their employees. Besides, the clients they care about are so uber-rich, they can afford to lose a few mil without blinking an eye."

"You can't combat evil by doing more evil!" Gabriel all but shouted.

Jubiel rubbed his chin for a long moment, then said, "Have fun commanding your self-righteous army of one, archangel." He sat down behind his table and picked up the cups that had fallen.

"What as in that bag Siren gave you?" asked Gabriel.

Ignoring the archangel, Jubiel started spinning his cups. I was so grateful Gabriel had bothered to ask a question, even if it wasn't a useful question, that I answered. "It's money. Martyr gives his winnings to Jubiel, who distributes them to non-profits."

Gabriel stared at me for so long I didn't think he was going to respond. Finally he said, "You're telling me that the field angels engage in illegal activities and give the money to charity."

"Not all the field angels," I said. "But the two you've met so far? Yes."

"Hey, busking is legal in London!" Jubiel said.

"Do we want to talk again about where the bean is?" I asked him, then I turned back to Gabriel. "I told you that you weren't going to like what you saw."

"Jophiel and Michael can't possibly know about this," Gabriel said.

"Oh, Jophiel knows. Why do you think he's stalled you for so long? Michael?" I raised a shoulder, considering. Michael wasn't my favorite person, but he did like order. I couldn't believe he would let the disarray of the field angels go on if he was aware how bad things had gotten. "Probably not."

"Why doesn't someone tell him? He could whip these malfeasors into shape, no problem!" A glint of Heavenly vengeance shone in Gabriel's eyes, which is not something I thought I would ever see.

"Ooh, malfeasors. Big word," said Jubiel. "Somehow I suspect if Michael cared at all about us little people, he'd have done something long ago."

Gabriel opened his mouth to respond, but I cut him off. I didn't want to listen to him argue with Jubiel all day. "Are you planning to get the flaming sword yourself and take out people for donating to charity? Because if not, I think it's time we let Jubiel get back to work and moved onto our next stop."

"Fenyx?" Jophiel gave a feral grin.

"Yup. I figured I'd start with the most agreeable of you and ease him into it. It hasn't worked in my favor so far."

"I think you're doing just fine with what you've been given." Jubiel gave Gabriel a pointed look.

Before Gabriel could say anything, I grabbed his hand. "On that note." I pulled the archangel back the way we'd come, not bothering to look back to see the look on Jubiel's face. I did toss a wave over my shoulder, though.

After we'd gotten out of the Square, Gabriel shook my hand off. "Do you seriously think they're doing the work the Lord intended?"

"Hey, you wanted to meet the field angels. I told you you weren't going to like it. I don't know what you want from me."

"I would like some evidence that if I made you my second-in-command, you'd be on my side in this and help me turn them into a force for good. Or recruit some other angels. Or something."

I stopped walking and looked him in the eye. "Well, if we're being all honest here—which you know is my best state—I don't think the 'sides' are the way you think they are. You're coming in and making demands of Martyr and Jubiel based on how you think Heaven and Earth work, but you have no idea. You've been gone for two thousands years, Gabriel. Things got pretty fucked up in your absence. Or probably more accurately, they were always fucked up. It's why you left, isn't it?"

Gabriel didn't say anything immediately. Instead, he grabbed my hand and pulled me to the alley we had first appeared in. "You may have a point," he said once we were in hiding. "So tell me what's really going on."

"No."

"No?"

"No." I tried to look determined but suspected I just looked tired. "I'm just your guide in all this. I'm not really a field angel. You want to know why they are the way they are, you ask them."

I couldn't read the look on Gabriel's face. I didn't know whether he was going to listen to me or argue with me again. Either way, I didn't want to hear it. I wasn't the one he needed to talk to. I reached for his arm and teleported us to an even smaller, darker space that smelled of disinfectant. I maybe should have given him some warning, because he immediately stepped into a bucket and knocked a broom and mop against the door with a huge clatter.

"Are we in a utility closet?" he asked.

"Yeah. Fenyx likes this hospital, but it's super open. This is the best place I've found to hide." I closed my eyes and switched my clothing to match the outfits of the cleaning staff, then stuck my head out the door. A doctor barely glanced at me as she passed, and after that, the coast was clear. "Come on."

We walked down the almost-abandoned hallway into a busier part of the hospital. After scanning the area, I led Gabriel to one of the rooms and stopped in the doorway. Inside, an East Asian family gathered around the bed of an elderly man. He was hooked up to any number of beeping devices, and his labored breathing suggested he didn't have much time left. The people surrounding him appeared to be his wife, daughter, son-in-law, and teenage granddaughter.

The man on the bed gave a stuttered gasp, and all the beeping machines blared as the patient's check stopped heaving. The wife put her hand to her mouth, and her eyes filled with tears. "Henry was going to be here any minute!"

The teenager, a girl dressed in a plaid skirt and jacket with emo makeup on her face, who until this point had been playing on her phone, leaned over and kissed the dead man's forehead. As she stood and moved toward the room's exit, the machines quieted, and the patient heaved another breath.

I pulled Gabriel to the side as a middle-aged man who bore a family resemblance to everyone in the room rushed through the door. The teenage girl slipped past him. "Am I on time?" the new arrival asked. "I wanted to see him one last time."

"Yes." The crying woman reached out to embrace him. "We had a false alarm just a minute ago, but—"

As she continued, I glanced down the hall to see a cadre of doctors and nurses hurrying toward us. I nodded in the opposite direction to indicate that Gabriel and I should follow the girl. "Is that—?" Gabriel cut himself off, shaking his head. "Did she—?"

I held my finger to my lips, and when the girl disappeared halfway down the hallway, I grabbed Gabriel's hand and pulled him through the ether after her. We emerged outside a house in what looked like the suburban United States. I couldn't quite determine the house's color because of the darkness of the hour, but the bright red blood seeping out of the man lying on the front stoop shone in the moonlight.

Fenyx knelt next to him and kissed him on the forehead. *I guess he had already bled out then,* I thought. The previously dead man, who appeared barely out of his teens, breathed in a huge gulp of air and began seizing. With no display of emotion, Fenyx stood up and walked down the stairs.

A man appeared in the doorway behind her. "Get out of here, little girl!" he shouted, brandishing a gun. "I—I'll shoot you too! I called the police! You hooligans can't come onto my property and steal from me!" He didn't sound nearly as confident as his words implied.

Fenyx didn't respond. She just continued down the sidewalk away from the man's house. I nodded to Gabriel that we should intercept her a few houses down, away from the police cars and ambulance blaring their way toward us.

Fenyx barely blinked as we stepped in front of her. No doubt she had been aware of our presence since the hospital. "Siren. Archangel. To what do I owe this honor?" If she conferred any honor on our visit, she didn't confer it to her flat tone.

"You... you brought two people back from the dead," Gabriel said, sounding astonished.

"Gabriel, meet Fenyx." I gestured at the girl. "The angel of the resurrection. Interestingly, she's also the only angel to have met Jesus in person."

"Unless you count Lucifer," said Fenyx with an indifferent shrug. "Are you going to answer my question?" She did not seem to care one way or the other if we did.

Gabriel should have explained our presence, but his flabbergasted expression suggested he wasn't going to be saying anything anytime soon. "Gabriel's taking over the field angels," I told her. "Something about mobilizing you all into a fighting force for good on Earth."

"Hm. I'll have to not consider that." She narrowed her eyes at me ever so slightly, and I had to believe she'd meant to offer a polite lie instead. Either way, she turned from us.

Gabriel grabbed her arm and spun her back around. "You have to be the most powerful angel I've ever seen! You're just a cherub?"

"Yes. Just a cherub. Who would like to be on her way." Fenyx's voice held none of the testiness her words implied. She also didn't fight against Gabriel's grasp.

"This is amazing!" Gabriel seemed happy for the first time since I had started introducing him to the field angels. "That family! I'm sure it brought them so much comfort to be together one last time! And that kid over there. I assume he was innocent of wrongdoing?"

Fenyx met Gabriel's gaze but otherwise didn't move. "Depends how you define innocent. He was going to steal a television and some jewelry. Hardly a capital offense. Now maybe he'll live, maybe he won't." She shrugged.

Gabriel dropped his hand from Fenyx's arm. "Then how do you determine who lives and who dies?"

"I don't," she said. "I find people who are dead and give them a few extra minutes. Sometimes it helps. Most of the time it doesn't."

Gabriel's brow furrowed. "How do you find the people you are going to bring back? Aren't there any number of people dying at any moment?"

"I just pick people," she said. "I try not to pick serial killers, but sometimes it's hard to tell."

"But if you focused!" Gabriel sounded excited. "You could find the most worthy people, or the ones most likely to be saved! You could do so much good with your gift!"

"Maybe," said Fenyx, though she didn't sound interested in the idea. "Or maybe I would prolong their suffering."

The creases between Gabriel's eyes deepened. "Then why do you bring people back, if you're not sure it's a good thing?"

"It's what I do."

"But if we could work together, we could do so much—"

"No, Archangel." Fenyx's voice still held little inflection, but the slight change in force brooked no opposition. "It is my gift. I will do with it as I choose. You cannot handle the responsibility."

I knew it was my time to interfere, and in my experience, Fenyx didn't do anything she didn't want to do. I had only known her to care about one thing, and I decided the best way to move this forward was to play my trump card before she abandoned this conversation entirely. "We're going to see Annie next."

Her head snapped toward me, and for the first time, her voice held a bit of emotion, a fierce protectiveness. "Leave Annie alone."

"No can do," I said. "Gabriel wants to meet all the field angels, which means Annie too."

I expected Fenyx to meet my gaze and try to gauge if I was bluffing, but she was a smart girl. She knew I didn't bluff. "Fine," she said, returning to her unaffected speech. "I'm coming with you."

CHAPTER 9

Bedlam

K HET AND I DROVE ALONG I-70 through West Virginia into Ohio. Or, rather, I drove, and Khet sat beside me and kept me company. The sun set shortly after we left the Archives, dimming my mood as well as the sky. It got dark so early this time of year in the United States—dark and cold and terrible. Ordinarily, when I got annoyed at the lack of proper light, I'd go somewhere else, but I could hardly teleport to Argentina or Singapore while I was driving. And of course, I had no idea what time it was in Singapore. I spread out my awareness to Asia, just enough to figure out if it was dark there.

"Watch out!" Khet sat straight up, and I came back to myself. The car bounced, and a grating noise filled the air as the left tires went over the rumble strip on the side of the highway. I jerked the wheel to right the car on the road, and we swerved back into our lane.

"What were you thinking?" Khet smacked my arm. "You can't teleport while you're driving a car! Especially one with me in it!"

I flashed her an apologetic look, but I was confused. I hadn't dematerialized. "I didn't teleport. I just sent part of my essence to Singapore."

"Well, whatever you did, you got all fuzzy and lost control of the car. Don't do it again!"

Well, that seems fair. "Do I usually get 'all fuzzy' when I teleport?" I asked.

Khet was silent for a moment. "No. No, you don't. Usually you just disappear. I was worried about you for a second, until you lost control of the car. Then I worried about myself." Her stomach punctuated her statement with a well-timed growl.

I laughed. "So, think it's time for some road trip food?" I asked, happy to change the subject.

Khet gave me a sideways glance, as if she knew I was avoiding her concern, but she said, "Oh, are you saying you had the foresight to pack sandwiches, then? Because somehow I doubt that, and even if you had, I'm smart enough not to eat anything you made. So I guess fast food would be the next most thematic option."

She was right. I hadn't thought to bring food along, and she probably wouldn't have wanted the peanut butter, Cap'n Crunch, and pickles sandwich I was craving. "We could stop at a grocery store and get pickles—I mean, sandwiches—for the rest of the trip."

"Nah, that's okay." She stretched in her seat. "Fast food is fine."

I made a face. "Fast food is gross."

"Coming from you, that's saying something," she said. "Come on! We're on a road trip! Embrace it!"

We pulled off at the next exit, where there was a King Wendy's or something like that. Khet and I each got some ginormous burger with all kinds of internally consistent fixings. I grabbed some sugar packets off the condiment table and shook them on my burger, but I was still disappointed at the lack of original culinary options. Khet had gotten onion rings, and when the greasy, bitter smell hit my nose, I decided her choice was wiser than mine. I reached out and traded her rings for my French fries.

"If you wanted onion rings, why didn't you order onion rings?" She ate a fry with exasperation.

"Well, I didn't realize I wanted onion rings until I saw you had them," I said. "I figured you had foreseen my desire and gotten them for me."

"And it didn't occur to you that I ordered them because I wanted them? Especially since you know I can't see the future?"

"But you know me. And see? You're eating the fries." I pointed as she put a second one in her mouth.

"Yes, because grease is grease, and it's easier than arguing with you and expecting anything to come of it. At least I know you won't steal my soda."

I wrinkled my nose. "I know. I don't get the Diet Coke thing. You're going to live forever no matter what you do. Might as well embrace the real stuff."

She shrugged. "I like Diet Coke."

"Khet." I looked her square in the eye, because this was serious business. "No one likes Diet Coke. Some people have drunk so much of it that they've convinced themselves they like it, but everyone secretly prefers regular Coke. Again, I don't know why you bothered."

She took a long sip of her soda and made exaggerated "Mmm" noises. I think she protested too much.

As we got back in the car, a thought struck me.

Aren't you trying to make Khet fall in love with you?

Oh, right. I forgot.

Do you really think she's going to fall in love with someone who steals her onion rings? After all, she fell in love with Gabriel, and the two of them are nice to each other to the point of lying about it.

Yeah, but what they have isn't real. Besides, stealing food works all the time in romcoms.

Romcoms aren't real either.

They're more real than Khet and Gabriel's romance.

Khet had dozed off in the passenger seat as I mulled this over. I got so lost in my thoughts, and the music blared so loudly, it took me a minute to notice the approaching blue and red flashing lights.

Oh, must be some kind of emergency, I thought, so I moved over a lane to let the vehicle by. When it followed me, I realized I might be in trouble.

Oops. I'm getting pulled over.

Don't you need, like, license and registration when that happens? That's what they always say on television.

Um. Maybe? I've never gotten pulled over before.

I considered speeding up and making the cop chase me. I could probably drive faster than he could catch up. I was a supernatural being with all the forces of chaos at my disposal, after all. Before I could, Khet roused herself and looked behind us. Suddenly she was wide awake. "Pull over. Now. Do not even think about running."

"But, Khet, what if it's one of those scams where someone pretends to be a cop but is really a psycho rapist?" Even as I said it, I slowed and pulled over onto the shoulder.

"Somehow I feel like you could handle it." Her voice was wry. I'm just glad you picked up that documentation I had made for you."

I put the car into park, then gave her a confused look. "What documentation?"

She blinked at me several times. "You are kidding, right?"

"Um..." I tried to guess what the right answer was. "Yes?"

"Oh, my God. You didn't." She rubbed her hands over her face. "Bedlam, you specifically told me you got the drivers license I had made for you in Philly. I asked you point blank, and you said, 'Yes, absolutely.'"

"Khet, you should know I'm always lying when I use the word 'absolutely.'" I tried to make light of the situation, but I could tell by the storm cloud of her face—or at least the red and blue flashing lights making her complexion look like thunder—that I was in serious trouble.

"Oh, God, this is bad." If she were bothering to use God's name in vain, she had to be upset. Usually she tried to pretend He didn't exist.

Someone tapped on my window, and I looked over to see a police officer standing by the car. I rolled down the window and gave him my best, brightest smile. "Is there a problem, officer?"

"Do you know how fast you were driving?"

He sounded awfully serious about it. Did he not realize that speeding wasn't that big a deal? Khet was still glaring at me and not giving me any guidance, so I decided the truth was probably my best option. "Um. Probably about 95?"

The cop blinked. Apparently honesty was not the normal policy in this situation. "You do realize you were in a 65 mile per hour zone, correct?"

"Honestly, I hadn't really thought about it," I said. "See, my philosophy on the speed limit is that everyone can control the car at a certain speed, and as long as you can do it safely, it's not a huge deal if you go above the limit. What's posted is really the lowest common denominator. Or numerator. I guess it's a numerator,"

I hoped the cop would either think I was funny or would be blinded by my amazing logic, but all he said was "Sir, I'm going to need to see your license and registration."

"Well, I have my registration." It was a brand new car. Even I hadn't had time to lose the paperwork the dealership had given me. "But I don't have a license."

The cop gaped. "You don't have a license, or you don't have it with you?"

I shrugged. "Pick one."

The cop opened his mouth even wider, probably about to tear me a new one, but Khet turned the charm up to nine hundred and intervened. "My cousin does have a license, sir. He just doesn't carry it with him. I've been telling him that's a problem for awhile." She managed to let out a disarming laugh and look ashamed at the same time. Her acting chops would have impressed me if I hadn't gotten fixated on what she called me.

Cousin? I don't want to be her cousin!

Be grateful she's not accusing you of kidnapping her.

"What's your name?" the cop asked me.

"Bedlam," I said. "What's yours?"

"His name is Brian Edward Lambert," said Khet. Her voice sounded calm enough, but I could hear the glower under her words directed at me. "He goes by Bedlam."

Judging by the cop's frown, my name wasn't winning any points with him. Policemen were all "epitome of law and order" types, and he probably thought I was some kind of anarchist, which I kind of was.

Hm. Maybe I should have picked up that license.

You think?

Well, I definitely would have if I'd remembered that Khet had asked me to do so.

"Sir, could you please step out of the car?' asked the cop.

"Don't you want to see my registration?' I asked, suddenly feeling cooperative. Very bad things could happen when a cop asked someone to step out of their car, especially when that someone looked as much like they might be from the Middle East as Khet and I did.

"I don't think that will be necessary."

"Sir, really." Khet's earnestness held a tinge of desperation. "He has the proper documentation, just not on him. We'll be happy to bring it down to the station in the morning."

"Good. You can do that. He'll be waiting for you there." The cop pointed at the ground next to him. "Step out of the car, sir."

"I really don't think—" I started to say.

"Bedlam," Khet said through gritted teeth. "Get out of the car." Before I could stop her, she pulled on the handle of her door to step out. Not wanting to leave her out there on her own, I followed suit.

"You don't need to get out, ma'am," said the cop, who still hadn't told me his name.

"Yes, I do," she said. "I can't drive, so I'm going to need you to take me to the station, where I can hopefully call a taxi to take me home to get his license."

He peered at her. "Don't you have a cell phone?"

She crossed her arms. "No. Not everyone does, you know."

"What would you have done if you had gotten into an accident, then?' he asked. "Which was bound to happen, given how he was driving."

"*I* have a cell phone," I said. That was a lie. I had lost my cell phone. But I could have teleported for help.

"Great," said the cop. "You can check it into evidence when you get to the station. Now, are you going to come quietly, or do I have to cuff you?" He seemed to relish the idea of the second option.

I, for one, didn't care. I had every intention of blinking out of the backseat of the police car and catching up with Khet later. I decided, though, that I would rather not become a police brutality statistic, especially since Khet had made it clear she had no means of recording my arrest. Besides, based on the way Khet was glaring at me, I didn't have a choice of whether to go.

The cop trundled us over to his vehicle as cars sped past us on the highway less than a foot away. Khet shuddered as each one went by, but I loved the rush. I considered running out in front of one of the cars. If the cop thought I was dead, he couldn't arrest me, though I would probably make a mess and traumatize some naive passerby.

The cop opened the back door of his car for me and watched me closely as I lowered myself in. "Front or back, ma'am?' he asked Khet.

"Back," she said.

I'm pretty sure that means she wants to lecture me.

Blah blah blah bring your license when you drive blah.

When the car door slammed shut behind us, Khet turned to me. "I *am* going to lecture you but not about what you think. You are *in no way* going to blink out of the back of this car. You are going to go down to the station. You are going to wait in a jail cell all night like a normal person, and tomorrow I will bring the documentation the policeman wants to see."

"Khet..."

"Don't you 'Khet' me. If you teleport out of here, I'm going to be here alone. He's going to think I helped you escape, and I'm going to end up in jail, which *I* can't blink out of."

"Okay, I'll just wait until I'm in the jail cell and you're far away," I said. "They won't be able to pin my escape on you then. They don't even have your name, and your Brian Edward Lambert doesn't exist."

"Bedlam, we were driving a car with plates. There's a paper trail."

"Paper trail?"

"Whose name did you register the car under?"

Oh. "Yours."

"Exactly. They're in the national system now. They'll be able to find me."

I shrugged. "So we run. We always run. You can go somewhere else, change your name. They'll never find you."

"I don't want to run, Bedlam! Not over a speeding ticket! I want to finish my degree. All you have to do is spend one night in jail. Can you please do that for me?"

Ugh. I really do not want to spend the night in a jail cell.

Especially since cops are jerks and might decide to keep me for longer.

But she said, "For me." How can I say no to that?

"Ugh, fine. But, really, we need to teach you to teleport. That would solve all our problems."

Khet did not seem amused. I suspected she was still mad at me. "We've tried. I can't. Besides. Paper trail."

Blergh. Why do you need a degree anyway?" I had aimed for a light-hearted joke, but my words came out petulant. She glared at me, then turned to look out the window. She didn't speak to me again for the rest of the trip.

When we got to the station, a squat, ugly building that matched all the appropriate stereotypes, Khet asked for a phone, then left me alone to be booked. They asked me all kinds of questions—my name, my age, my profession. I had no idea what answers were already on the ID Khet had made for me, so I went with the truth. I think they were ready to let me go by reason of insanity, except they didn't want crazy people driving.

After the interrogation, they took my picture. I stuck my tongue out at the camera for the front shot but was obedient for the side. I figured if I was half good, Khet would only hate me for half of forever. After what felt like hours, they brought me down to a room full of iron bars comprising connected cells. Each had an uncomfortable-looking cot and a wash basin. I had a momentary hope that I could at least talk to the person in the cell next to me, but apparently no one other than me had gotten caught committing a misdemeanor that night, because all the other cells were empty.

My eyes felt heavy, so I lay down on the cot and tried to sleep. It didn't work out so well, partly because the mattress was apparently made of lumpy rocks and partly because I didn't sleep well without Khet beside me. I gave it my best shot, though. I tossed. I turned. I fluffed my crappy pillow. I just couldn't fall asleep. Eventually I gave up. I sat up and looked around. The only person in residence was a lone guard at a desk at the end of the row of cells. For more my benefit than his, I yelled out the thought that was running through my head over and over.

"Bored!"

CHAPTER 10

Michael

N o, *NO, NO, NO, NO.* The word repeated in my head faster than I could count, so I had to number them in retrospect. *Five no's. Neither auspicious nor inauspicious.*

Numerology was a lie. The situation was dire. I could not be trapped here with Lethe. I tried to teleport out, praying to the Almighty my angel powers worked in this section of the caves. Lucifer must have denied my Lord access to these caves as well, though, because I remained in my human form. I paced around the small cave like a madman, pulling at my hair with my fingers, then staring at them as they came away covered in blood.

"Oh, my Michael." The smile was gone from Lethe's face, replaced with an expression of worry. "Don't you see? You need to rest. You need to heal. When you're better, I'll let you go."

I laughed, and the unsteady, too-loud sound echoed through the space. "Lethe, if you let me out, I can heal myself. I'll take forever to heal at human speed."

She gave me a placid smile. "I know. And I will nurse you and tend your wounds and take care of you. By the time we're done, you'll love me again. You'll let me return to Heaven."

"Lethe, you don't—" I couldn't counter her insane logic. I didn't know where to start. I had no power to allow her back into Heaven. My sword had damned her, but only the Lord could grant that forgiveness. Bedlam was the only angel to return to the Lord's grace, and he had died to save another for that privilege. If I'd had my choice of demons to return to Heaven, Bedlam would have been at the bottom of the list.

I could explain that efforts to make me love her again were pointless. I already loved her. I couldn't stop. I didn't want to be with her. She was an evil demon, and even if she had not been, our relationship might not have worked out in the long run. She had never been strong, mentally or physically, and while she could lean on my physical strength, I didn't have the emotional capacity to support both of us through a relationship. When we were together, I did all I could to keep it together for her, the same as I did for Heaven. I had begun to think if I had the opportunity to fall in love again, I'd need someone who could see all my weaknesses and still love me. An image of Cain came unbidden to my mind, but I shook it away. I had treated her terribly for millennia. She could never love me, even if I were free of this demon in front of me, who was no doubt dreaming up new ways to torment me.

I stopped pacing, and Lethe came forward to rub her hands along the cuts on my arm. The stinging sensation made me focus on her, though I suspected she was trying to comfort me. *Only Lethe would think digging her fingers into open wounds would comfort someone.*

"My poor Michael," she said. "I will get some bandages to tend you."

"Lethe, for Light's sake, I don't need bandages! I need—" As I spoke, she disappeared before my eyes. "—to get out of here!" I let out an aggravated growl. I wanted to swipe out at the place where she had stood, but despite my warrior background, I generally didn't hit people. *Except demons. Which she technically is. But she's my demon. Even though*

I don't want her to be. I clenched my fists and stared up at the ceiling, then rolled my head around.

My eyes landed on the lever that triggered the portcullis. She had left me alone with it, which meant I could escape. I might have to wander the caverns for eternity, but I was good with directions. I remembered which way we had come, so I needed to wander in new directions until I found a place I could teleport out of. If I hugged the left hand wall, I should eventually find a way out.

I tugged on the lever, expecting it to give easily under my physical strength. It didn't budge. I looked around its base for some kind of locking mechanism, but all I found was smooth metal. I pushed and pulled at it several times to no avail. Lucifer's magic must have allowed it to work for only Lethe.

I glanced at the portcullis itself. Maybe I could lift it and get out that way. I crouched down beside it and grabbed hold of a bar near the bottom with both hands. I tugged upward with all my might, the iron burning into my sensitive flesh. The metal gate rose the barest millimeter, then clanked, metal against metal, refusing to rise any further. I stuck my fingers down in the holes beneath the prongs, and while I knew nothing about gate design, I suspected some kind of locking mechanism secured the portcullis. I could not escape that way.

Frantic tears came to my eyes as my breaths came faster. How had this happened to me? How had I gotten trapped, completely out of my element? I thought back to finding Asphodel in that dark alley, and I realized that only my own hubris had brought this on me. I had thought I could fight demons endlessly without repercussions, but of course they would take vengeance eventually. What sweeter revenge could there be than putting me at Lethe's nonexistent mercy? I could not trust myself around her.

My fault. My fault. My fault. I needed to keep myself together. That's what I did, after all. I held myself upright, certain of the righteousness of my cause. The trouble was, I was never certain of anything, and as soon as I realized Cain was not my enemy, I had lost any sight of my mission. I didn't know if she was an agent of good, or if she was tempting me down a dark path, and I didn't care. I was no longer sure of anything, and I was trapped.

I counted the bars on the portcullis. *One, two, three, four, five...* All the way up to eighteen. Three sixes again. Three sixes, even in the land of the woman I loved. Whom I did not want to love. Who could bring me no comfort. I padded out a rhythm of seven with four of my fingers. *Pinky, ring, middle, index, middle, ring, pinky. Pinky, ring, middle, index, middle, ring, pinky.* Over and over again I counted, trying to forget the eighteen bars on the portcullis, as well as my left out thumb.

Eventually, blessedly, I blacked out.

I stared at the place where Bedlam had turned to smoke on my sword for long enough that Raphael prodded me. "Um, Michael? Do you want me to step into the circle?" The teen angel was sweating, as if he were concerned he might be condemned along with the others. Even I knew such an idea was ludicrous. I would betray Heaven before innocent Raphael would.

When God cleared him, and I asked him to step out of the circle, he breathed an audible sigh of relief. I called upon Beelzebub next. The jovial angel's betrayal had surprised and wounded me. He had always been the most good-natured of us, and the realization that someone so pleasant could also be evil did not sit well with angels.

"Well, hello there, Michael," he said, his deep voice full of cheer as he stepped into the flames. "Lovely day we're having here in Heaven. Shame it's the last I'll see of it."

"You made your own choices," I said.

"So I did. So I did." A red sigil appeared above his head. "I can't say I regret them, though perhaps time will show that you do."

I stayed my blade for a moment. "Regret my actions, or regret yours?"

Beelzebub laughed, and the flames made his eyes appear a diabolic red. "Regret everything, Michael. Regret everything."

I heard a chuckle to my left, and I glanced to see amusement on Lucifer's face. I didn't know what the joke was, but I suspected it was at my expense. I shouldn't have let them laughing at me affect me, but I was an imperfect being. I regretted driving my sword through Beelzebub's chest less than I might have a moment previously.

Rachel and Nathaniel both passed the test. I then called on the seraph whom I had most expected to fall but who had remained stubbornly loyal through all the battles. Her katana of light had cut through more renegades than Rachel's had, though I doubted the warrior angel knew that. "Siren."

The petite angel stepped into the circle with a sneer on her face. "Yes, let's get this facade over with. You don't need to test me. You know I can't lie."

No sigil appeared above her head, and the spot just above my temple that hurt in reaction to the exact pitch of her voice lamented it. "The question is not whether you believe in your innocence but whether God does."

"Well, does he?"

I sighed. "No."

"Exactly. Try not to sound so disappointed." She stepped out of the circle and went to join Sybil and Somniel without being asked.

I hated this role God had forced upon me, that of executioner, if not judge and jury. I could almost feel the metaphorical chains around my wrists. *No, that doesn't make sense. I don't want to break free. To break free would mean to defy our Lord, which I would never do. Never.*

"Oo-roo-loo-roo-la." I awoke to a tuneless melody in my ear and a gentle touch on my face. "Oh, my MIchael." I opened my eyes to see Lethe, still polished and put together, cradling my head. "You are awake. I'm afraid this is going to sting a little." She placed a damp cloth against the wound on my head.

I cried out as she rubbed at my cut. Apparently she had fetched peroxide or rubbing alcohol—or some kind of poison—because whatever she used stung to high Heaven. I shot upward out of her reach, banging my head against the wall.

Lethe's eyes shone with what looked like pain, though I couldn't be certain my suffering didn't bring her pleasure. "Lamb, you need to hold still. I can't clean your cuts otherwise."

I cringed at the use of her old nickname for me. She had only ever used it when we were alone, and I hadn't heard it in millennia. "I don't need you to clean my cuts. I need you to let me out of here."

"Michael." She stood up and rested her hand against my face. "I can't let you go. I need you to love me first. If you love me, you'll save me."

Maybe it was my muddled head, but she wasn't making sense. "I don't understand."

"You condemned me to Hell," she said. "You weren't wrong to do so. I wasn't worthy of your love then. But I am now. I am! So now you can save me."

"Lethe, I..." I was ashamed to hear my voice tremble. "I didn't condemn you to Hell. I would never have done that. I simply acted on the Lord's wishes. He's the only one who can redeem you. Not me."

"You... you never would have damned me on your own?" she asked.

"Well, I guess 'never' is a strong word," I said. "But I never wanted to turn you into a demon, no. But you have to understand that it's not my choi—"

"You love me," she whispered.

I paced around the room, running my fingers through my hair. "Of course I love you. I'm an angel. I can't stop loving you. It doesn't change anything."

"It changes everything." She took a few hesitant steps toward me. "Don't you see, Michael? As long as you love me, there must be something in me worth saving. And you and I, we can work out our issues. You don't have to be strong around me. She came even closer and reached out to wrap her arms around my neck. "You never were before. You let me see your weakness."

I froze. "Who are you?"

Something in my expression made her pull her arms back before they touched me. "I don't understand," she said. "I'm Lethe, your love."

"No, you're not." I took a step back from her. "Lethe never saw my weakness. She was the weak one. She needed my strength. I could never tell her how badly I needed her too."

"Michael, your head is injured. You're remembering all wrong—"

"No, I'm not." Something wasn't right. Something was off. I just couldn't figure out what it was. I just knew that this person in front of me was not Lethe.

Words popped into my head. "I can dig around in there. I can find your worst nightmares and make them real. I can create your wildest fantasies and keep you trapped in them for as long as I like." Asphodel had said that, and I understood. Lethe had never rescued me. I was still chained to that God-forsaken wall with the three-sixes of chains on either side.

"Asphodel!" I screamed, ignoring the phantom Lethe, who pleaded with me even as she faded from sight. "Get out of my head!"

Demonic laughter echoed through the chamber as it expanded around me. I could once more feel the cool rock against my back and the hard iron around my arms. The noise dimmed to a point to my left, and I saw the Prince of Lies, waggling his fingers as if conjuring some kind of spell.

"I wondered how long it would take you to figure out it was me in there," he said. "But I have ammunition now, and I think we're going to try something different for the next phase." With that, he took his lantern and sauntered out of the cave, leaving me with nothing to do but hurl curses at the darkness.

CHAPTER 11

Siren

THE SUN HAD LONG SINCE set, so I felt comfortable teleporting to Annie's apartment door. She lived on the twelfth story of a high rise with an internal door, and I figured after the day I'd had, I was entitled to scare a human or two who was dumb enough to be up at this hour. I moved to knock at the door, but Fenyx glared at me. I stood aside and made a sweeping gesture, indicating she could do the honors, if she insisted. With a delicacy that probably surprised Gabriel, the only person who knew Fenyx and hadn't seen her with Annie, the emo angel knocked on the door.

"Annie?" she asked. "Are you sleeping?"

"Door's open," came a child's voice from inside the apartment. Without a sound, the door slid open under Fenyx's gentle touch, and Gabriel and I followed her inside. The stupid apartment was dark except for the light coming off a computer screen, illuminating a girl who looked to be about ten, with light brown pigtails tied up in pink ribbons. "You know I don't sleep, Fenyx."

"You're not supposed to be on the computer," said Fenyx. "You know it overwhelms you."

The girl didn't turn away from the monitor. "Don't chastise me in front of Siren and..." She cocked her head, as if listening. "...the archangel?" She turned around to gape at Gabriel, then looked at Fenyx. "What is the archangel doing here?"

"Outlook remains cloudy," said Fenyx, dropping back into her accustomed sardonic voice. "But I think he's trying to fix us."

"'Us' as in the field angels?" Annie blinked, considering. "Are we broken?"

"Well, anyone who thinks Martyr's not broken isn't paying attention," said Fenyx. "But I think the rest of us are doing fine."

Gabriel cleared his throat. "You're not working as the field angels are intended to work. You're supposed to get a list of prioritized requests from the prayer center and answer them." His voice was gentle, as if talking to a child. I rolled my eyes. Annie may have had cute freckles and a puppy on her shirt, but she was as old as the rest of us.

"Oh." She turned back to the computer in a clear gesture of dismissal. "We can't do that. Jophiel stopped sending us orders centuries ago."

"Wait, what?" Gabriel opened and closed his mouth a few times, each time starting to speak, then changing his mind. "How do you know what prayers to answer then?"

"I watch the internet," said Annie, as if that explained everything.

"Annie's the angel of awareness," I said. "She can't help but pay attention to literally everything that goes on around her. Which is why she mostly stays in a dark apartment with the lights off."

"She should stay off the internet, too," said Fenyx under her breath. "It overwhelms her."

Annie gave an exaggerated child's sigh. "*Everything* overwhelms me. If I sit in the dark, I can still hear things. At least this way, I'm useful."

Gabriel looked from Annie, to Fenyx, to me, then back again. "I don't understand."

Annie typed a few words on her keyboard. "I compile things I find, and if there's an emergency, I let the others know. Like right now, I think Beelzebub is trying to steal Christmas."

Fenyx and I spoke in exasperated unison. "Again?"

"What do you mean, 'again'?" asked Gabriel.

Fenyx shrugged. "Beelzebub tries this schtick every few years. He picks a metropolitan area and recruits some human mooks to break into people's houses and steal all their presents."

"Every few years? Why haven't I heard about it before?" Gabriel said.

I opened my mouth to explain that it was sort of a Christmas tradition for the field angels, but Fenyx spoke before I could. "I don't know, archangel. Maybe it's because you've been ignoring anything and everything related to your responsibilities for the past two thousand years, and you can no longer recognize what people doing their job looks like."

"Fenyx. Not helpful," I said. She gave me a bland look. She knew as well as I did that she couldn't say it if it wasn't true.

"Siren, may I have a word?" Gabriel's voice was testy. He didn't wait for me to respond before he grabbed my arm and dragged me toward the entryway of Annie's studio. I thought about pointing out that Fenyx and Annie would still be able to hear anything we said, but since I wasn't big into secrecy, I decided not to bother. "Explain. All the things you wouldn't tell me before. I want to hear them. *Now*." His words held the command of an archangel, and I was reluctantly impressed. I therefore decided to be straight with him, instead of snarky.

"These are the field angels: Martyr, Jubiel, Fenyx, and Annie." I took a deep breath, pondering what to say. Gabriel must have thought I was going to shut him down again, as he looked about to chastise me, but I held up my hand. "There used to be more. There used to be a lot more. But one by one they did something to piss Jophiel off—argue with him, handle a situation in a way he didn't approve of, wear the wrong color shoes, whatever—and he'd assign them to the prayer center to punish them. Eventually the only field angels left were the ones Jophiel couldn't control."

"Couldn't control." Gabriel's voice was flat.

I raised my shoulders in a helpless shrug, willing him to understand. "Annie and Jubiel went to the prayer center for awhile, but Annie couldn't handle the inundation of human thoughts. Jubiel couldn't be in the same room as Jophiel without arguing with him. Both of them got sent back to Earth. Fenyx scares the shit out of Jophiel. Martyr flat-out refused to go to the prayer center, and no one can beat him in a fight."

"*You* beat him in a fight."

"Yes, but I'm not inclined to make him go. Anyway, these four, Jophiel gave up on, and they've been the field angels ever since."

"So they're useless. I'm in charge of a team that doesn't follow orders and doesn't do their jobs." Gabriel spoke these words to himself, but then he focused on me. "And you knew. You've known all along."

"They're not useless! Martyr and Jubiel raise money—"

"I've met Martyr and Jubiel, remember? They're just a cage fighter and a con man."

"No one is 'just' anything. They're angels, and better ones than most of Heaven's so-called leaders."

Gabriel made a scoffing noise in the back of his throat. "I don't have time for this. With Michael missing—"

"Whoa, whoa, whoa! What do you mean Michael's missing?"

Gabriel rubbed the bridge of his nose. "It means I've looked everywhere on Heaven and Earth for him, and I can't find him."

I blinked a few times, trying to process the information. "If Michael's missing, why aren't you looking for him? Why isn't everyone in Heaven looking for him?"

"I didn't want everyone to panic!" Since he said it in my presence, he must have believed it was true, but I was having a hard time seeing the logic in it. "I gave Bedlam the task of finding him."

I blanched. "Bedlam? You put Bedlam on it? The most irresponsible demon-slash-angel to ever set foot in the celestial realms? The being who hates Michael more than anyone else in creation, which we all know is saying a lot? What were you thinking?"

"I was thinking that Bedlam has powers no one else does, and he might be able to use them to find Michael." Gabriel's voice rose in volume with every word. "And I was thinking that you had offered to introduce me to the field angels, and I had no idea how long that offer was open for."

"Seriously? You thought I'd rescind my offer because you needed to deal with an actual emergency?" I was practically shouting now, and I didn't care. "What do you take me for?"

"I take you for the least trustworthy of Heaven's angels."

I flinched at his words. I didn't know whether he had meant to say them or whether the combination of momentum and my power had forced them out of him, but I could not deny that he believed they were true.

"You claim to be the angel of honesty." His voice was softer now but no less angry. "Yet everyone you get close to ends up corrupted."

Tears stung the corners of my eyes, and I hated my own weakness. I wanted to argue with him, but I couldn't, because deep down inside, I wondered if he was right. "If you hate me so much, why did you agree to make me your second in command?"

"I was desperate!" The words burst out of him, and he had the good sense to look ashamed. "I was desperate," he said, more softly. "But I'm not anymore. There are no field angels to work with, so I'm just going to have to come up with another solution. At least that means I don't need to make you my second-in-command."

"You said." I realized it was the response of a child, but my head was swimming too much to come up with something more mature. "You said if I introduced you to the field angels, I could be your second-in-command. I told you that you weren't going to like it. You can't take it back now. You can't."

"Forget it, Siren. I don't have time for your patheticness. I need to find Michael. And save Christmas, apparently."

"How do you plan to do that?" I asked, the bite back in my voice. "Jophiel isn't going to give you any resources."

"I'll call Rachel in."

I felt the blood drain from my face. "What?"

"Rachel's got a whole team of warrior angels who do nothing but train all day. It only makes sense to recruit them to be the field angels Heaven so thoroughly needs."

I grabbed Gabriel's arm. "Don't do that. Don't call Rachel in. There's a reason even Michael knows better than to activate her."

Gabriel shook off my hand. "There you go again. 'Even Michael.' You don't trust anyone in Heaven, so why should we trust you?"

"Gabriel, seriously. If you call Rachel in, she'll—"

"I am tired of your mysterious lack of explanation for how things 'really work' in Heaven. Rachel has a team of competent angels, and they're better equipped to handle anything than you and your lot." Without another word, he teleported out.

I thought about following and railing at him, but I suspected he was done conversing with me. Besides, if Michael was missing, and Gabriel was getting Rachel involved, I had a limited amount of time to solve everyone's problems before things got really bad. I glanced back at the main body of the studio to find Fenyx and Annie staring at me, having obviously eavesdropped on the argument. *Not that "eavesdropped" is the right word for listening to a shouting match.*

Part of me considered talking to them and soliciting their help in solving these problems. But the truth was that I wasn't a field angel, and they only trusted their own. I was on my own, as I always had been, and I needed to save the world.

CHAPTER 12

Bedlam

JAIL WAS LITERALLY THE WORST thing ever. I had nothing to do. The food was terrible even by my lax standards. The cop on duty kept glaring at me like I was some kind of hardened criminal, not some guy who'd been caught driving without a license.

It's not like I don't have a license. I just didn't have it with me.

Actually, you don't have a license.

Eh. Khet forged me one. That counts.

Does it?

The guard had a small radio playing the local country/ western station, and I needed every ounce of my willpower not to change the station. I didn't have a problem with country music, but my instinct was always to choose my own soundtrack. However, the fact that Khet would find a way to kill me if I let my otherworldly nature get out made me sit through the commercials.

I couldn't blink out to refresh myself, so I did sleep eventually. I had weird dreams in which my cell phone screen cracked and a club played 90s music on 80s night. I woke up in the morning to the most disgusting porridge I had ever eaten and waited for Khet to come get me.

The shift change brought new music—oldies this time—and I once again tried to strike up a conversation with the guard to no avail. My own thoughts were my only company. I wondered if most people were comfortable with their own thoughts, as I was not. I had too much nasty stuff in there: Keziel, the war, Hell, my time as a demon, and a whole slew of other things I tried not to think about. I had happy memories, too, but when I was by myself with only the voice in my head, I ended up back in places I never wanted to visit again.

Maybe you should, like, write songs or a book or something to distract yourself.

Like I have the follow-through for that.

It really doesn't help that "Sympathy for the Devil" is playing right now.

Eventually, I sang along with every tune on the radio, much to the annoyance of the ungrateful guard. I wasn't the best singer in the world, but I had tremendous gusto. My voice was a little hoarse by the time, a few hours later, the phone next to the cop rang. He spoke a few perfunctory words I couldn't hear over the noise of my own baritone, then hung up. His keys jangled on his belt as he approached me.

"Looks like you're getting out of here." He identified the correct key without effort and unlocked my cell.

"Thank the Light!" I bounced up and down in anticipation of fresh air and human companionship, then sprung out of the cage as soon as the door opened enough to let me through. The guard rolled his eyes as if he were just as glad to be rid of me as I was to be rid of him. We took the elevator up, and I whistled a melody until I realized it was Lucifer's favorite song again. I made some gagging noises, and the guard looked at me as if I were nuts. I ignored him and leapt out of the elevator when it opened on the main floor of the police station. I bounded over to the beautiful and perfect Khet standing in front of the desk.

Or at least I tried to. A different cop stopped me. "Hold on. We still need to outprocess you." He then led me over to a table. "Now, your cousin brought your license, but you were still going over—" I tuned him out as he droned on about court dates and fines and community service. Instead, I studied Khet. She looked pretty, with her hair tied back in a ponytail and circles under her eyes as if she hadn't slept well. She also looked bored out of her skull.

See? We are soulmates. Neither of us slept well, and we're bored of this place.

Um. She's probably still furious with you.

I'm sure it's fine. She never stays mad at me.

I wouldn't bet on that.

Eventually the cop handed me back my personal effects—also known as my car keys—and let me go over to Khet. I planned to say something. I don't know what, but I'm sure it would have been funny or clever or at least uniquely me, but before I could, she gave me a cold look and walked out the door.

Oof. Still mad then.

Told you.

It's okay. I can work with this.

You can work with the silent treatment?

"Come on, Khet." I didn't mean to whine as I followed her out into the brisk air, but I didn't mean to do a lot of the things I did. "You can't stay mad at me forever."

"Maybe not," she said as she ducked into a taxi she had apparently kept waiting there. "But I can stay mad at you for right now."

Wait, why is there a taxi? Where's the car?

You left it on the side of the highway, dumbass.

"Does it help that I'm really sorry?" I asked as I sat down next to her. "I should have listened to you when you said to pick up the license."

"You should have listened to me both times I told you to pick up the license. And no, it doesn't help, because you're going to do the same thing again. You drag me off on this trip to God knows where—possibly quite literally—and you keep getting distracted. Don't you have a mission?"

"Ehhhh." Finding Michael wasn't really at the top of my priority list, and I didn't think it would be at the top of Khet's either.

"I can't deal with you right now. Can we just not talk for awhile?" Khet turned and stared out the window.

"Okay, but this isn't just about the license, and you know it." I said it to goad her into talking, but as the words came out of my mouth, I realized they were true. She was mad about the mission and not knowing what it was. She was angry with Gabriel for being neglectful. She was probably mad at herself for not handling these things better, but she wasn't just mad at me.

We made it back to the car in about 10 minutes, and it was right where we left it. My beautiful new baby hadn't been towed or impounded or stolen or crashed into or anything. I could have kissed the hood. Who knew I'd be so attached to a car?

After making sure Khet buckled up, I merged into traffic and headed for California. I didn't put on the radio in hopes that the actual silence would make Khet talk, but when she finally said something, it didn't sound like her, and it wasn't what I expected

"What the fuck do you think you're doing?"

I looked at Khet, but she looked just as surprised as I did, so we both turned and glanced at the backseat. A tiny figure with straight, shiny hair sat there, her blue eyes looking like they had a personal vendetta against me. I was about to ask what she was doing there when the car hit the rumble strip.

"Watch the road, you moron!" Siren gripped her door handle.

"Hello, Siren. How can we help you?"

Khet had apparently decided to try to catch flies with honey this morning, but Siren had always been more of a spider. Siren, in the typical manner of an angel who didn't care about humans, ignored Khet. "Bedlam. You're supposed to be looking for Michael. I fail to see how you can possibly be looking for him on a highway in the middle of Ohio. He's not anywhere around here."

I didn't expect the sharp intake of breath from Khet. "What?" she asked. "Michael's missing?"

I knew Siren wouldn't respond to Khet, so I took up the conversation. "Relax, Siren. I have a plan. Or, rather, I have Gabriel's plan. I'm headed to California to find Lethe. We're hoping my-slash-Azrael's power will help me find him."

I expected Siren to call me on my bullshit. She did not, as a general rule, pull punches. To my surprise, Khet spoke up first. "Michael's missing and you're wasting time going to museums and spending the night in jail?" She sounded angrier than I'd ever heard her.

"Hey, you're the one who said I had to spend the night in jail!"

"Don't you dare turn this around on me!" Her eyes flashed, her cold annoyance from before a distant shadow of the fiery rage I found myself confronted with. "You are the most irresponsible—" She cut herself off and glared out the window again. "Pull the car over."

"We just got back on the road." I don't know what effect I was going for, but i was pretty sure lighthearted banter wasn't going to cut it this time. "I promise we'll drive straight there from now on. I've got my license this time."

"It'll take us at least two days to drive there, and you can teleport there in two seconds." Khet turned back to face me, and her brown eyes had a hardness in them I didn't think her capable of. "Pull. The. Car. Over."

I did as she commanded. I wasn't going to argue with those eyes. As soon as I stopped the car, she got out and slammed the door, then started down the side of the highway.

I got out too. "Khet!" I called after her. "At least let me give you a ride somewhere first! It's not safe on the highway!" She kept walking, and I swung myself back into the car, intending to follow her until she got back in.

As soon as I moved to press the ignition button, Siren grabbed my arm. "You need to find Michael. You may be the only one who can."

I shook off her hand. "I don't care about Michael. I do care about Khet." I didn't start the car, though.

Siren gave a dismissive wave. "She'll be fine. She can't die. Michael, though..." She looked like a lost little girl. "I don't think he can die, but maybe..." She shook her head and her expression hardened. "Just find him. He's not my favorite person either, but he's the only one who can keep Jophiel under control."

"I don't want to get pulled into Heaven's politics," I muttered, though I realized I didn't have a choice. I stretched out my awareness, looking for Lethe. Her position hadn't changed since I started this mission. I let out a heavy sigh and teleported out.

CHAPTER 13

Michael

I SLOUCHED AGAINST THE WALL WAITING for Asphodel to return, though I wasn't sure I would know if he did. He might have made me believe he had left when he never had. I counted the tears that slid down my cheeks, always in multiples of seven, or so I told myself. I was too tired and despondent to fight against my chains any longer. No doubt my spirits would rally again, and I would flail against the shackles, but for now, I wallowed in the blessed silence.

At long last, Asphodel returned, and when he did, he carried someone in his arms. I could only make out the barest hint over her form from on top of the lantern that also hung from his hands, but she had long hair and a simple dress.

"Look who I found wandering the streets of Ohio." Asphodel righted the figure and snapped her into the chains adjacent to mine.

I could make out her dusky skin, and I knew once her eyes opened, they would be a luminous brown. "Cain?" My voice came out in a rasp. *It's not real. It can't be real.* I looked Asphodel in the eyes with as much confidence as I could muster. "You're playing games with my mind again. It's not her. Cain lives in Maryland, not Ohio."

"Does she?" Asphodel lifted her limp head, as if getting a glimpse at her face would help tell her address.

"Perhaps it was Maryland, then. Humans change their borders with such frequency, it's impossible to keep their location names straight. Suffice it to say, I decided actual torture was unnecessary—you've done plenty of injury to yourself—and fooling you with your lover was really giving up my best internal material already. Physically torturing someone you care about? Now, that sounds like fun."

"You can't torture her." I almost growled the words. "She's under Lucifer's protection."

Asphodel's laugh echoed through the cavern. "You must want to protect her a great deal to invoke his name. Suffice it to say that he's given me free reign in this matter. I can't kill her, of course, but so many things are much worse than death."

I took as deep a breath as I could under the circumstances. Cain's presence might be another trick, but I couldn't risk her harm if it wasn't. "Let her go. Do whatever you want to me. Just let her go."

"Oh, Michael. I know I can do whatever I want to you. You might even enjoy it. I've never seen a more broken mind in my life, and I've been called on to make Lethe behave. The two of you really are perfect for each other. Doing something to her, though?" He nodded at Cain. "*That* would torture you, and thus better suits my purpose here."

He hummed to himself for a moment, then pulled out a long, thin, green stick from his belt. "Do you think bamboo under the fingernails is a bit cliche? Maybe so, but it is effective. Besides, I'm enough of a demon to appreciate the classics." He held her hand up and ran it along his cheek. "Let's see if we can't wake her up."

I could picture having bamboo slice my fingernails from my hands, and the very thought had me cringing and shaking my hand to make the image go away. The idea of Asphodel inflicting my punishment on Cain made my knees buckle.

With the same deliwwwcacy as his smooth words, Asphodel lifted Cain's hand and ran his bamboo stick over the tops of her fingernails like a file. Then he lifted her middle finger and slid the edge of the bamboo under the lip of her nail. I couldn't watch. I whipped my head away and scrunched my eyes shut. A feminine whimper sounded to my left, followed by an all-out scream.

"What the—?" Cain gave an anguished gasp. "Asphodel?"

My head snapped back toward Cain. My gaze stayed on her face so I wouldn't have to see her bleeding hand. "You know Asphodel?" *Of course she does. She knows all the demons. She's friends with them. She's corrupting you even now.* I silenced the racing thoughts in my head. If Asphodel had kidnapped and tortured her, they could hardly be friends.

"We met in Hell a few months ago." She glanced down at her arms, and I couldn't stop myself from looking where she did. We both gasped at the iron chains encasing her wrists and the blood oozing from her right hand. "What's—what's going on?"

"We're playing a little game," said Asphodel in a sing-song voice. "I call it 'How much can we hurt Michael?' Research suggests threatening you causes him pain, and like any good scientist, I needed to test that theory."

She was staring at me, so she didn't react when Asphodel lifted another of her fingers. When the bamboo went under her index fingernail, she howled in pain and tried to rip her hand away. Asphodel held fast, and her only achievement was a spatter of blood on her perfect face.

"Leave her alone, Asphodel!" My voice had most of its usual timbre back but didn't match the voice of command I could usually manage for Heaven's angels. His only response was a diabolic smile and the removal of another one of Cain's nails. She and I flinched in sync. She didn't scream, though, and I worried she had passed out, but her brown eyes remained focused on my face. "Stop it! Hurt me! Torture me! Leave her alone! She's done nothing!"

Asphodel tsked. "Hasn't she? I mean, she hasn't been running around the world sending demons to Hell, but despite certain demons' fondness for her, she's always been on Heaven's side. Did she not redeem Heaven? Did she not send Sybil and Somniel to the abyss?"

"I'm on the side of Earth, you idiot," Cain said.

"Earth isn't a side." Asphodel flensed another one of Cain's fingernails, and this time she let out a small scream. I instinctively reached out a hand to her, but she was just out of my reach.

"It... is a... side." She gasped the words, and I admired her ability to continue an argument in the face of torture. "Hell tries to corrupt us, and Heaven mostly ignores us, but Earth still has lots of people just trying to make it through the day."

Asphodel sneered. "Angels count. Humans don't."

"We do matter!"

Asphodel dropped Cain's hand and turned away, and I fell back against the wall in tangible relief that he was done with her, at least for now. Then he spun around again, grabbed her other hand, and drove the bamboo under two of her fingernails in quick succession. Her anguished roar filled the cavern.

"They don't," said Asphodel. "*You* don't. The war is between Heaven and Hell, and Earth and its residents are just another battleground. You're lucky anyone cares at all what side *you* pick, little girl."

Asphodel turned his gaze on me then, and I could feel his dirty fingers probing around in my mind. I knew I should focus on helping Cain, but there was nothing I could do to stop the world from falling away again.

The next angels on my judgment list were Mephistopheles and Lilith, Lucifer's two strongest lieutenants, of whose fortunes I had no doubt. Mephistopheles stepped into the circle first. He looked around at his fellow angels and must have realized there were almost none from his side left in Heaven. Nonetheless, he made his plea. "I ask all of you to reconsider. Why follow a God who cares nothing for us? He made us as the first of his creations, when his ideas were flawed. Immortality. Eternal love. An essence made of one alleged virtue. He abandoned us in favor of his less perfect but more balanced human race. Why should we be forced to serve those who came after us? Stand with those of us who refuse to be seen as lesser creatures because of the flaws of our Maker!"

The crowd murmured, and I wondered whether his words would sway anyone. He had hinted at them in the heat of battle, but never had I seen his argument laid out in such a plain and civil manner.

Siren spoke first. "You speak of the flaws of our Maker, as if He should own up to them, but he has never claimed to be perfect. Maybe instead of calling him out, you should look to your own flaws and acknowledge your own mistakes. They cause you more harm than anything He has done to you."

Mephistopheles sneered. "I expect nothing else from you. You believe our lives should be suffering."

Siren flinched as though he had slapped her. "You know that's not true."

"I can't lie in your presence." A mocking tone laced his words. He turned to me. "End this, Michael. I am tired of fools who can't see the truth when it smacks them between the eyes." I obliged with little of the regret I felt for the other angels. Mephistopheles had always been a problem.

Lilith stepped into the circle, and I gave her a moment to speak. She simply stood, tall and proud, as she faced her doom. I glanced at Uriel. Rumor had coupled the two of them for centuries, but I could not see his face to know if it betrayed any emotion. With a shrug, I ran my greatsword through Lilith's chest and let her body turn to smoke.

Looking around the room, I breathed an internal sign of relief. The ordeal was almost over, and Lucifer should be the only angel I had left to condemn. I raised my hand and beckoned my beautiful Lethe, my lucky number seven, into the circle. She took the few steps with a trepidation I attributed to fear of the fire, but I did not worry. Many of the loyal angels had feared the encircling flames or the outcome of the trial. I gave her a reassuring smile, and when she smiled back, a peace settled over me for the first time that day. Then I looked up and saw the red symbol floating above her head.

"What did you do?" Before I knew what I was doing, I had crossed through the circle of flames and grabbed her by the arms. *"What did you do?"*

She looked up at me in shock and horror. "Michael? What's wrong?" I didn't have to say anything. She knew only one thing could make me react the way I had. "I don't understand. I fought for Heaven. I fought for Heaven!" She addressed the last words not at me but at the ceiling, at the God who had condemned her as surely as I would have to.

"You did." My voice had become cold and distant, and I dropped her arms. "I know you did. I saw you. Yet God condemns you. So I ask you again. What did you do?"

Tears streamed down her cheeks, the glistening trails flickering in the firelight. "I didn't do anything."

I stepped backwards out of the flame. "Siren, get over here!" I braced myself for the usual barrage of complaints about being used as a lie detector, but Siren must have been capable of some empathy, because she simply came to stand behind Lethe. The flames must have burned her, but without a word or a cry, she put her hand on the quivering angel's shoulder.

"I didn't do anything," Lethe said. "I just... I knew. Before the war, I knew Lucifer was thinking of rebellion, and I didn't tell you. I promised... I promised I would ask for mercy for them if they lost."

I thought back over the last few weeks. Lethe had in fact asked for mercy for the rebels. I had attributed the request to her gentle soul, not the growing cancer of evil I realized was growing inside of her. I nodded to Siren, who removed her hand and stepped back. My emotions resembled a tornado tearing up my insides, but I turned my external facade to hard granite the winds of my anger and despair couldn't penetrate. I raised my sword.

"Please Michael!" Lethe dropped to her knees. "How could I do anything else? I am mercy. It's what I am! You cannot condemn me for that! You cannot!"

"It is not I who condemns you," I said, forcing myself to meet her gaze. I didn't want her to see how thoroughly she had shattered me, and knew that the twin pieces of ice that had become my eyes wouldn't show the hurricane within. "It is the Lord." I swung my sword and watched as the woman who could be my love no longer turned to smoke as black as my heart must be.

Gabriel placed a hand on my arm, though I did not look to see whether he condemned me as well. I told myself I still had one brother by my side, and nothing would take him from me.

I opened my eyes to find myself back in the cave. Asphodel had gone but had left the lantern this time, and I found it something of a relief to be able to see my surroundings. I looked to my left to see Cain hanging from the chains, or at least half-hanging. Her hands were a bloody mess, but one of them was free of its shackle, and she seemed to be concentrating very hard on the second.

My breathing must have changed, because she looked over at me. "Michael! You're awake! I'll be right over." She winced as she pulled her left hand free of the iron that encased it.

"You got out," I said as she walked over to me. Her feet were bare, and I wondered if Asphodel had stolen her shoes to prevent her from escaping.

"The cuffs were designed for someone with bigger arms than mine. It took me a few tries, but I got out."

"Great." My voice sounded harsh, but I meant the positive sentiment. "Now get out of here, before he comes back."

She ignored me and looked me over, frowning. "You're hurt."

"Not as hurt as you," I said. "And definitely not as hurt as you're going to be if you stay."

She waved a blood-caked hand. "I heal quickly."

"Not down here you don't. These caves negate angel powers."

She gave me a wry smile. "They negate most angels' powers. Not Lucifer's, and he's the one who gave me the fast healing. I'm more worried about getting you out of here. I wish I knew how to pick locks."

Why was she dwelling on me? She was the one in danger. "Are you listening to me? Get out of her. Asphodel's going to torture you if you stay."

"He'll torture *you* if I go!" Her words came out laced with frustration and desperation. "I can take a few torture sessions. They aren't my first, and they won't be my last."

I shook my head. "Not torture like this. Asphodel has powers. He can make you see things that aren't there. He takes your deepest fears and desires and uses them against you."

She looked me square in the eye. "There is nothing in my mind that scares me. There is something I don't understand, though. Why am I here? What purpose does torturing me serve?" Her expression was unreadable.

I swallowed. "He thinks torturing you will hurt me."

She looked at me for a long moment, her gaze never leaving mine. "Will it?"

My mouth was dry. I didn't want to admit it, but I couldn't hide from her. I nodded once. "Yes."

She reached out and laid her hands on either side of my neck. I flinched. I couldn't help it. I didn't like it when people touched my neck. "I'm not going to hurt you, Michael," she said, though she moved her hands down to my shoulders.

"I know. I just—"

"Shh. It's fine. I understand."

She did. I knew she did. She could see all of me and didn't judge me. In that instant, I knew the truth of why I had hated her for so long. I hadn't believed she was evil, not really. I was simply afraid of someone seeing past all my defenses, because I knew she could use it against me. Looking at her, with her bright brown eyes gazing into mine, I didn't know why I'd ever been afraid. She would never intentionally hurt anyone. She would never intentionally hurt me.

"This is a bad idea," she said, and I barely had time to register what she meant before she stood on her tiptoes and her lips met mine.

CHAPTER 14

Siren

L EAVING BEDLAM'S CAR ON THE highway seemed gauche, so I drove it to the nearest town and parked it outside a gas station. It might get towed at some point when someone realized the owner wasn't actually patronizing the place, but I didn't really care. I wasn't sure why I had bothered to move the car in the first place.

The tallest building in town seemed to be about three stories tall, and I decided that would suffice. I teleported myself to the top and looked out over the cars, whose owners were in a surprising rush for such a sleepy town.

What am I going to do about Beelzebub? I needed to handle the situation before Gabriel got Rachel involved. Gabriel was probably going to have to do a fair amount of convincing to get the warriors to do anything, as unused to productivity as they were. Or maybe they'd be excited to have a job at all. Maybe I was already too late. Either way, I couldn't handle the situation on my own. I could beat up a handful of Beelzebub's mooks, but he'd likely have more than a few. I could call the police and make the thieves tell the truth in my presence, but in my experience, cops weren't very helpful with planned crimes, only executed ones.

I continued pondering my options until I heard someone walk up behind me. I expected a maintenance man to yell at me to get off the roof, but instead a compact, muscular figure sat down next to me on the lip of the building.

"Hey, Lor," said Martyr.

"Still not my name," I said, not bothering to look at him. "They let you out of the cage?"

He lifted a shoulder, then let it sag. "I do leave occasionally. Why so glum?"

"Do you want the long version or the short version?"

He spread out his hands. "I've got nothing but time."

I took a deep breath and started at the beginning. Not the actual beginning, of course. Martyr was well aware of my life story. I told him about Sybil and Somniel leaving and my desperation to find a place I belonged in Heaven. I described how I had lied with my actions and how I didn't know what that meant. I confessed to how badly I had screwed up introducing Gabriel to the field angels, as well as my ulterior motives for helping the archangel in the first place. "And I still need to figure out how to save Christmas!"

Martyr stared at me in silence long enough for me to grow self-conscious. Eventually he said, "You're not a liar, Lor."

I looked directly at him for the first time since he had sat down on the roof. I didn't know how he had cottoned onto the one thing that was bothering me more than anything else. I hated not belonging in Heaven, and I was furious with myself for how badly I had messed up the field angel introduction, but my bad feelings had started when I used my actions to lie to Rachel. His conviction should have convinced me. After all, he had to be telling the truth, but how could he know me better than I knew myself? "Aren't I?"

"We can't live as perfect examples of our virtues all the time," he said. "I mean, I get pummeled for charity on a regular basis, but it's not like I'm donating my organs and letting them grow back. I take breaks, and I haven't died for anyone yet."

"It's not the same," I said. "I can't lie. I've never been able to before."

"You didn't lie, Lor. Or, if you did, the lie was saying you wanted to be a warrior in the first place. You don't like or respect them, and you did what you had to do to stay true to yourself."

"Maybe." *Maybe.* "But that was still a lie."

"You of all people should know that the truth is complicated," he said. "You wanted to join on some level, and you didn't on a deeper level. Both can be true at the same time."

"I guess," I said. Some of the weight on my heart eased, but I still felt heavy. "But that doesn't change anything else. I still don't belong anywhere."

Martyr's favorite smirk graced his face. "We might have something to say about that."

"We?"

Another figure appeared on my right hand side. "Give us a smile, love."

"Also not my name." I glared at Jubiel. "You guys need to stop calling me 'Lor' and 'love' and anything else that begins with 'L-O.'"

A childish giggle materialized into Annie on Martyr's other side. "I am only calling you 'Lollipop' from now on."

"I hate you all," I said.

"See, there you go thinking two things at once again," said Martyr. "You don't really hate us." By the time he was done speaking, Fenyx had appeared next to Annie but hadn't said anything. Apparently I wasn't getting a new nickname from her.

"We've been talking," said Martyr. "We've decided you can be one of us."

I blinked, looking at each of the field angels in turn. Fenyx looked as bland as ever, but Annie and Jubiel both had encouraging smiles on their faces. "One of you?"

"Only if you want," said Annie in a rush.

"And you can't be our leader or anything," said Fenyx. "We don't need a leader."

"But we're the misfits of the angel world," said Jubiel. "We do field angel work as best we can—"

"Though not to the satisfaction of *some* archangels," said Fenyx under her breath.

"—and we figure you do pretty much the same thing," said Jubiel. "You'd fit right in."

"Besides, we could use someone who has some clout in Heaven," said Martyr.

I barked a laugh. "I don't have any clout in Heaven. They hate me up there."

"You got an archangel to meet with us," Jubiel said. "Which admittedly we didn't react well to. But none of us could even have gotten his attention on our own."

"Rumor has it you yell at Michael on a daily basis," Annie said. "None of us has the guts to do that. Well, Fenyx might be brave enough, but she never yells. Or cares."

I took a deep breath. A warm feeling was rising up in me at the idea of belonging to a group that actually wanted me around, but I couldn't get too excited yet. "What does joining you entail?"

Martyr's smirt intensified, as if he had won a bet. "Nothing you don't already do. We're the agents of Heaven who actually give a damn about Earth. All you have to do is keep fighting for the little guy and help us out with the occasional big mission."

I let out a breath. "And Gabriel?"

Martyr's smirk fell. "What about him?"

"He means well. He really does." I didn't know why I was pleading his case. He really didn't deserve it. But I had a feeling his jerkiness the past few days was rooted in the same cause as mine. "I think he's as lost as any of us. He just doesn't realize it."

The group exchanged glances. "If he comes back, we'll think about it," Martyr said. "Like Jubiel said, we know we fucked up with him."

"He's gone to get Rachel to help with the Beelzebub situation," I said. "You know what that means."

Annie grinned. "How about we show him how useful we are and handle the Beelzebub situation ourselves? That'll save Rachel from having to get involved."

"We have a plan," said Jubiel. "We could definitely use you."

"Is my job to stand next to people and make them tell the truth?" I asked.

"Hell, no!" said Jubiel. "We need you to punch things!"

"You're going to have to tell me about this plan," I said. "I don't see Martyr and I taking out Beelzebub and all his goons on our own."

"Well, you'll have my zombies to help," Fenyx said. Four heads swiveled in her direction. "Kidding." She didn't sound like she was joking, but then, her deadpan voice made her very difficult to read.

Jubiel rubbed his hands together. "Okay, so here's the *real* plan..."

CHAPTER 15

Bedlam

I FOUND LETHE AT A SOUP kitchen in L.A. She had told me she wanted to earn her way back into Heaven, so I suspected she was there to help the homeless. However, instead of dishing out gruel to the line of people stretching out the door, she sat at one of the tables and conversed with a despondent-looking man in rags.

"So you see, it's very simple." Her musical voice sounded almost sane, until you listened to her words. "If you've lived a virtuous life, you can end your own suffering and go to Heaven. It's beautiful there, all full of shiny gold clouds."

I facepalmed. If her idea of getting back into Heaven involved driving the virtuous to suicide rather than sinners, she still had a long way to go. I took a seat next to her. "Or, you know, you could continue to live a good life here on Earth, where I'm sure things will start looking up for you any day now." I gave Lethe a pointed look. "May I have a word?"

I didn't wait for her to respond before I grabbed her arm and teleported her out to the alley. When we rematerialized, I let go of her arm, pushing her toward the wall. "I thought you were trying to get back into Heaven. Do you really think your same tricks are going to do that for you?"

Lethe looked up at me with deep, black eyes that nonetheless managed to look soft and pleading. "I'm

122

helping him, Bedlam! He's a good man, and I'm going to get him into Heaven."

"I don't—" I cut myself off. "I can't—" I started again. "You don't even know what's past Uriel's door, and—" I ran my fingers through my hair. "You know what? I can't deal with your brand of crazy right now. I need your help."

Her face lit up. "You need my help? Is it with an angelic mission? I want to help Heaven so much! Tell me what I can do!"

"Michael's missing, and I need you to—"

"What?" She shrieked so loudly that a few passersby on the street glanced into the alley.

I really should have seen that coming.

You'd better back up a bit. Stand far enough away so no one thinks you're mugging her and gets heroic.

I leaned against the opposite wall and let her get her rending and wailing out of the way. "My poor, poor Michael! How can he be missing?" She darted forward and clenched my shirt in her fists. "You must find him, Bedlam! You must!"

Hey, be careful with that! It's silk!

Don't worry about your shirt. Worry about calming her down.

I hate being the voice of reason. It's really not a role that suits me.

Oh, and leave out the bit where you spent two days ignoring the mission.

"I'm trying to find him. That's why I'm here." I intended my words to be soothing, but I sounded annoyed. "Gabriel thought if I found you and used Azrael's power to look at the fake Michael over your shoulder, I could maybe find the real Michael."

She stopped crying and looked up at me. "Your power works like that?"

Um. No. "It might. I can try it."

"Then do it." Lethe spread her arms out to the side and lifted her gaze toward the sky. "Read my love. Find him."

I turned on my power, and a stoic Michael appeared behind Lethe's shoulder. Even looking at this pale shadow of him made my toes twitch, but I ignored my inherent dislike of him and studied him, trying to connect to the real Michael. The echo in front of me, though, was simply a manifestation of Lethe's desire.

No wonder Azrael was such a bitch. Her power was completely useless.

I don't know about that. She used it to pretty good effect.

Lethe's beatific pose dropped. "Did you find him?"

"No," I said. I could see the tears forming at the corners of her eye again, so I rushed to continue. "But maybe you can still help me. Do you know of a place where Gabriel wouldn't be able to feel him, other than the Haven?"

Or Hell.

Yeah, not mentioning that possibility.

Her mouth formed a perfect "o," and her whole face lit up. "I do!" She smiled and clapped her hands. "Lucifer has a set of caves in the Appalachian mountains where he's blocked off angel powers, like he did in the Haven. Michael must have found them and gotten lost. He'd never be able to find his way out. They're a total maze."

"Or maybe Lucifer brought him there for some reason?" My reason made more sense to me than Michael taking a spelunking holiday.

"That doesn't seem very likely." Lethe's tone was blithe. "Lucifer doesn't want Heaven to know about the caves." She gave me a sideways look, as if remembering I was an angel, albeit the least Heavenly one. "I'd better go look for him."

I stepped closer to her. "You're taking me with you."

She winced. "Lucifer would be oh-so-angry if I did that. He'd be mad already if he knew I'd even mentioned their existence."

"But you don't answer to him anymore, remember?" I tried to sound as reasonable as possible. "And Michael could be injured. You'll need my help getting him out."

She wrung her hands. "I still don't know—"

I took a menacing step forward. I couldn't physically hurt her in any way, but she had always shrunk in the face of an imposing figure. "Lethe."

"Oh, all right!" She grabbed my hand, and before I knew it, we were at the entrance to a cave. The surrounding mountain was green and covered in trees, but the cave itself was made of blue-grey stone.

I ducked inside and walked a few hundred feet to where the cave split in three directions. I turned back to Lethe and almost stumbled over her, so close was she on my heels. "Which way?" I asked.

She eyed each of the tunnels and moved her fingers as if she were calculating something or, more likely, trying to remember which path led where. "I don't know. I can't feel him. I can't feel anyone in this cave. I don't know why he came, so I can't know which way he went."

Without thinking, I did something I hadn't done in the two days since Gabriel had told me Michael was missing: I reached out with my mind and tried to find him.

Why are you bothering with that? You can't find him. Everyone says so.

Oh, right.

Guess we're in for a cave exploration adventure, then.

Seems that way. Except... wait.

Michael had always been the easiest angel for me to find, because the forces of chaos in the universe, from which I drew my powers, avoided him like the plague. I didn't have time to shut down my automatic searching before his presence made itself known to me. He was nearby, somewhere to the right.

How can I find Michael? Lethe said angel powers are blocked here.

I dunno. Maybe he's your evil opposite. Does it matter?

Nope. Let's just find him so we can end this nightmare of a road trip.

"Come on." I nodded my head at the right-most tunnel. "He's this way." I started in the direction I indicated.

"Are you just pretending to appear confident?" Lethe's tiny feet pattered unevenly behind me, trying to keep up with my longer gait. "Because there's no way you could possibly know that."

"I know, but I do." I quickened my pace. I didn't want her asking more questions I couldn't answer, especially when the uncertainty terrified me.

CHAPTER 16

Michael

C AIN PRESSED HER LIPS AGAINST mine and twined her arms together behind my neck. I froze for an instant, unsure what to do. I didn't love her—*couldn't* love her—but something about her warm body pressed against mine made me want to feel more of it. I shifted my body ever so slightly forward, enough to return the kiss.

I didn't pull her closer. I didn't dare. I worried anything I did might drive her away, and I couldn't face that. No matter my feelings, I realized I desperately wanted her to love me. If she, whom I'd maligned for centuries, who had turned out to be the person I needed more than anyone, could love me, I had hope for redemption. I could perhaps break free of the prison in my head and learn how to be a decent angel who was capable of leading the host of Heaven.

I hated my own selfishness. How could I want her to love me when I couldn't return the feeling? But guilt didn't stop me from opening my mouth for her when she pushed to deepen the kiss. Her tongue laced with, and for a moment I let her sweep me away to a place where I wasn't a hopeless wreck stuck in a demon's dungeon. For a few precious seconds, I was someone who deserved love.

A demon had locked me in a dungeon, though, and I couldn't forget that completely. Asphodel had brought her down here too, and I needed to get her out. Gabriel would collapse on me again if she died.

Gabriel. The knowledge of my own wrongdoing had not been reason enough for me to break this growing connection between myself and Cain, but the realization that I was kissing my brother's wife was enough to pull my mouth back and rest my forehead against hers. "We can't," I said. "Gabriel."

She let out a sigh so sweet I nearly captured her lips with mine again. "I know. You're right. I just..."

I pulled my head back so I could see her eyes. "You just what?"

She tore her gaze from mine and shook her head. "Nothing. You're just right." She stepped back, unlacing her arms from around my neck. "Your wrists look terrible. We should wrap them in something."

The chains on my arms clanked as I grabbed her shoulders. "No, you should get out of here before Asphodel gets back."

She lifted her chin, and her eyes hardened. "I'm not leaving you alone down here." She ripped the left sleeve off her shirt and tore a strip off.

"Cain, he ripped out your fingernails. I don't want to think what he'll do nex—" I broke off as my gaze fell upon her bare left arm. I needed a moment to place what was wrong with it, but I shouldn't have. Her skin was a smooth, unblemished brown, which was both a beautiful sight and a grave error on Asphodel's part. The real Cain bore a scar above her elbow where I had marked her with my flaming sword eight thousand years ago. It was the symbol of her damnation, and I had placed it there. If it was gone, that could only mean one thing: The woman in front of me was another phantom of Asphodel's.

"Get away from me." DIsgust rose in my chest as I realized I had kissed this illusion. I hoped the embrace had happened in my head and I had not kissed Asphodel.

I had no issue with men kissing men, but I had a huge problem with me kissing a demon. "You're not her."

"Michael, what are you talking about?" She reached forward to wrap one of the strips of fabric around my wrist, but I yanked my arm back. She flinched to the right, and I could see that the mark of Cain had appeared on her upper arm where it belonged.

Was it always there? DId I miss it before? I shook my head. I would never forget the presence of my greatest shame. "Leave," I said. "Or go back to your chains. I don't care which. You aren't real."

Tears formed in the illusion's eyes, and it looked so like Cain that I wanted to comfort it. I had appeared implacable in the face of worse threats, though. "Fine," it said. "But I'm not leaving you. I'm going to chain myself up again. Let me know if you change your mind and want your wounds bound."

I closed my eyes, unwilling to look at the phantom. I didn't trust myself not to cave and believe that she was there with me. If Asphodel tortured this thing that looked so like Cain again, I could not bear it, but if I ignored it, he might move onto some other ploy. I leaned my back against the cold stone and prayed to be anywhere other than where I was.

Uriel and Keziel passed the test of the flame with flying colors, in that their tests happened in a blur I would never be able to remember clearly. Lethe's loss had set my thoughts spinning, but after Keziel returned to Jophiel's side, I had to focus. The hardest task was now before me.

The other angels had worn their traditional white robes as they faced judgment, but as my brother Lucifer stepped into the circle, his robes shifted to the deepest ebony. He stood not tall—he had always been the shortest of the archangels—but proud, seemingly unaffected by the carnage he had wrought. If anything, he seemed pleased.

"Have you any last words before I send you to your fate?" I focused on keeping my face implacable, and I was proud that not even my lip quivered as I stared down my once-fellow. In my heart of hearts, though, I longed for him to offer some explanation for what he had done. He arched a single eyebrow as he looked me up and down, and I tampered down my desperate thoughts. Somehow I had forgotten he could hear my inner monologue.

"Oh, Michael." His rich baritone diffused through the room. I could sound commanding if need be, but I didn't have the power to make my words seep through the very essence of a room and soak into the skin of listeners as he did. "You don't understand. I could make it a surprise, but we are brothers, are we not? I suppose I can do you one last favor before we are forever enemies. I can explain the truth to you."

"I know the truth." No one left in Heaven would find a trace of doubt in my tone, though of course Lucifer could read my own self doubt. I performed not for him but for the angels I found myself in charge of. "You have lost this war, and the consequence is eternal damnation." I used the word the Lord had for the punishment of the rebels. It was a new word, and I knew nothing of its meaning except that it was a curse.

Lucifer's lips turned upward as he shook his head. "Do you honestly think I went into this war not knowing what the outcome would be? I got plenty of information from this 'Lord' you worship while he thought I was his dutiful little slave. I wanted to take over Heaven, of course, and force him out of our lives, but I knew that was unlikely. He is more powerful than I, after all. So I settled on the next best thing: my own realm in the Abyss."

"There's nothing in the Abyss." I spat the words, and again, only Lucifer knew my anger covered for the spinning thoughts inside. *Lucifer planned this? He knew he was going to lose? Has he been ten steps ahead of me this entire time? Of course he has. He always has been.* "It's nothing but darkness."

"Mephistopheles likes to say we angels are mistakes, but despite his erudite nature, he's always had a penchant for the dramatic," said Lucifer. "The truth is we are beings of great celestial power, and the universe gravitates toward us. We can create our own realms around us, or at least the seraphs can. We will make something of this nothing, and our domain will be far greater than this gold shrine you cling to."

I stepped forward, ready to slash this being I no longer recognized through the chest. "This conversation, like the war, is over."

"Oh, no, Michael." Lucifer's face bore the same placid smile it had since he'd stepped into the circle. "The war is just beginning. I'm merely changing the battlefield. You angels like to claim your job is to shepherd the souls on Earth, and I have discovered you are right. We draw spirits to ourselves, and while we've all congregated here, the human spirits rise to Heaven. But now there will be two centers of gravity, and souls more aligned with my wishes will find themselves in my domain when they shuffle off their mortal coils."

Beside me, Gabriel gasped. "You're going to condemn them to the Abyss."

Lucifer's teeth gleamed in the light as his grin became feral. "So like my youngest brother to state the obvious. You want the human souls to go to their 'proper rest'? You're going to have to fight for them. And let's be honest, Michael. You're going to lose. You don't have what it takes to go up against me. You may be able to bluster the rank and file, but you and I both know you aren't up to the task of leading the host. I look forward to watching you crumble."

His words had given me pause. I didn't understand why the Lord would allow me to condemn angels to the Abyss knowing their presence there would doom his favored creations. I wondered briefly whether imprisoning him here would somehow save the poor mortals who had become as caught in this web as I. But I had already sent enough angels to the Abyss that the "centers of gravity," as Lucifer called them, must have already shifted. Besides, the "rank and file" needed a show of strength. They needed me to follow through on God's wishes, not question whether our Lord was even on the side of Heaven. With a cry of rage, I struck down my still-smiling brother, damning humanity, and perhaps myself, in the process.

CHAPTER 17

Siren

I TOUCHED THE BLUETOOTH COMMUNICATOR IN my ear. I didn't like it. Technology was so annoyingly human. Angels lacked telepathy, though, so we needed the devices to know when Annie was in place.

"Stop sighing like that, Lor," said Martyr. I could hear his smirk even though I couldn't see him. "You're loud enough to give away our position."

"I'm on a freaking roof across the street," I said, even though I knew he was teasing me. I felt a small smile of my own on my lips. I hadn't been teased in a very long time. "I very much doubt anyone's going to hear me from here."

"Stop talking, or you're all going to give us away" came Fenyx's cool voice over the comms.

"Good. You're back," I said, trying to peer into the boarded-up warehouse that was our target. According to the information at Chicago's city hall website, the building was abandoned, but Annie had tracked Beelzebub's operation there. "Did you get what you needed?"

"Of course."

"I still don't know how you got Rachel to give it to you," I said.

Fenyx muttered something about being good at her job, and Jubiel laughed. "Rachel's afraid of Fenyx," he said.

"Everybody's afraid of Fenyx, except us, and we have no qualms using that to our advantage."

I shifted my gaze from the warehouse to where Fenyx crouched on a roof several buildings away from me. I wondered whether being an outcast among angels bothered her as much as it did me, but i couldn't see her expression, not that it would matter if I could. Her face no doubt remained as cool and neutral as ever. But then, she had found her place among Heaven's misfits a long time ago, and my association with them was still tenuous at best.

"We're good to go then," I said. "Annie, you can get into position."

"You're not the boss of me," she said, but she disappeared from the roof across the way. A few moments later, she whispered, "Okay, I'm in place, and the fat man is in the building." Translation: She was in the rafters of the warehouse, and Beelzebub was on site.

"Hey!" said Jubiel. "It's not okay to fat shame anyone, not even an archdemon."

"Mentioning his weight isn't fat shaming," said Annie. "You're taking social conventions about size and ascribing them onto what I said. It would be more fat shaming to pretend his size didn't exist."

"Guys," I said. "Focus. What's the layout, Annie?"

"Seven hundred twenty-six boxes stacked in a maze. Fifty-three guys here, spread out among the boxes." She gave a list of empty spaces in the building. "Beelzebub is on the catwalk on the west side. Fifteen feet up, about twenty feet from the side of the building. You could see his back from the central window there if it wasn't boarded up."

Fenyx nodded, so I assumed she had enough information. I wasn't close enough to see movement from Jubiel, but he would speak up if he had issues. "You're up, Jubiel," I said.

"On it."

"Okay, Jubiel's in. The ladder to the catwalk just rose, apparently of its own accord." Annie whispered a play-by-play of Jubiel's antics, spilling crates and tripping people, then disappearing before they knew what happened. Annie's mic picked up the occasional terrified scream, until finally a dark voice yelled out, "Jubiel!"

That was Fenyx's cue, and she didn't need me to tell her to go before Beelzebub moved. "She's taken him out with the light blade," said Annie. I could picture what the people in the warehouse must be seeing, their all-powerful boss disappearing in a puff of smoke, replaced by a much smaller avenging angel wielding a glowing dagger, a sick smile on her face. "Sometimes I think there's something wrong with you, Fenyx," said Annie. "Anyway, they're running toward the door. They'll arrive in three... two... one..."

I teleported inside the building, right by the workers entrance. The warehouse also had a loading dock, but Jubiel had jammed the door from the outside before we started this. Martyr appeared beside me. He glowered at them and cracked his knuckles, while I gave them a fierce grin.

"You're supposed to be good cop, Siren," said Annie in my ear. "Why do you look like you want to eat them alive?"

I tried to sweeten my smile but probably failed. I'd told the team that Martyr might have looked more like a thug, but he was still the pleasant one. "Okay, here's the deal," I said. "We put our champion against your champion. If you win, we'll go away, and you can continue your sinister plans, admittedly without your illustrious leader. But if we win, you hand yourselves over to the police without a word. Any takers?"

In a perfect world, the men would have argued amongst themselves about who the champion was, and maybe knocked a few of each other out along the way. Earth, though, was no more perfect than Heaven or Hell, and these individuals—mostly men but a few women as well—sized up Martyr's and my short statures and decided we came up lacking. "There are fifty of us—"

"Fifty-three," Annie whispered in my ear.

"—and two of you. How are you going to stop us?"

I glanced at Martyr, and he shrugged. We lowered ourselves into fighting stances and prepared for the onslaught. Ordinarily, fifty-three on two would have been bad odds for Martyr and me, but the narrow opening meant we could only fight six or seven at once. Since Beelzebub never hired the smartest or best trained mercenaries, the two of us could handle those odds with ease. I had never fought alongside Martyr, only against him, but we knew each others' tells so well that the translation from opponent to ally happened naturally. He knew when I would duck and he could get in a surprise punch, and I anticipated when his uppercut would allow for a fortuitous kick. In less than two minutes, fifty-three unconscious minions lay in a pile on the floor.

"They really should have picked a warehouse with more exits," said Martyr as he cracked his knuckles again.

"I would have thought unboarding the windows would have been easier than going through the two of you." Annie flipped herself down from the rafters and landed in a crouch on the catwalk.

"I found some incriminating documents." Fenyx saved a stack of papers as she appeared behind the heap of people.

"Let's call the police and skedaddle," said Jubiel, appearing beside her. I nodded, and Martyr and I stepped over the bodies to join Fenyx and Jubiel, as Annie performed another acrobatic stunt to get down to ground level next to us. That position—the five of us standing over fifty-three beating victims—was exactly the one Gabriel, Rachel, and a slew of warrior angels holding steel blades found us in when they kicked open the door.

CHAPTER 18

Michael

RUNNING FOOTSTEPS HEADED TOWARD ME as my consciousness returned to the cavern. My eyes darted around the empty space. Cain was gone, if she had ever been there—*No,* I told myself. *She hadn't—* and Asphodel lounged against the opposite wall, a bored expression on his handsome face. I turned my head in time for my bleary vision to take in Bedlam and Lethe rushing through the entrance.

Bedlam? Lethe? Here? Together? That doesn't make any sense. I shook my head, trying to understand the purpose behind this illusion. Was I supposed to imagine that the former demon was having an affair with my ex? That was even less likely than Cain kissing me.

Asphodel began a slow clap that echoed throughout the chamber. "I wondered when you would bother to show up. Not that I minded the slowness, of course. Torturing an angel is such an exquisite joy." He smacked his lips.

Lethe ran over to me. "Oh, my poor Michael! What have they done to you?" She threw her arms around my neck. I shuddered when I remembered that only a short while ago, I had felt Cain's illusory arms do the same thing.

"I'm fine," I said, trying to pull back from her, though her iron grip and the rock wall behind me made distance impossible. *If it even is her.*

137

Bedlam remained in the mouth of the tunnel, taking in the scene. He met my gaze and arched his eyebrow as if to ask if I was okay, but that must have been my imagination. Getting no response from me, he turned to the demon in the room. "What's your game, Asphodel?"

"My game?" Asphodel's expression was innocent, but the depths of his black eyes could never seem anything but tainted. "It's not my game. Now that you're here, I suspect the maestro will come to explain himself. Ah, there he is now."

A shift in the air made me whip my head to the right, no easy task with Lethe's arms still clamped around my neck to see a being wearing an impeccable suit and holding a skull-topped black cane. He'd made no noise as he arrived, but his presence filled the room. I didn't need to look to know that every eye had turned toward him. Such was the power of the devil himself.

"Lucifer." Bedlam and I growled the name in unison, then turned to glare at each other.

Lucifer arched a single eyebrow at us, as if our synchronicity warranted a moment of consideration, then turned his attention to Asphodel. "Thank you for your excellent service. You may go."

A slow smile crept up Asphodel's face. "I look forward to claiming my reward."

Lucifer's brow furrowed, but everyone knew his look of confusion was an act. "And what reward would that be? Is not the pleasure of serving me reward enough?"

Asphodel's head reared back. "Oh, no. No. You agreed that if you did as I asked, you would grant me sovereignty over Azrael's realm."

"Did I?" Lucifer's eyes widened in an approximation of innocence, but even he could not keep the small smile from gracing his lips. "I think if you search your memories, you'll find I made no such promise."

Asphodel's face grew redder as he no doubt ran through his past conversations with Lucifer in his head. I almost pitied him, for I too knew what it was to fall victim to Lucifer's games. "You bastard," said Asphodel.

"Sticks and stones, cherub." Lucifer turned to me and Lethe, dismissing the lesser demon.

"You will rue this day, Lucifer," said Asphodel, and before Lucifer could turn back to the Prince of Lies, if indeed the devil had any such intention, Asphodel blinked out.

Lethe turned her head from where she had been sobbing on my shoulder. "Why are you doing this, Lucifer? Why are you hurting my Michael?"

Lucifer looked me up and down, and I tried to imagine what he saw. In my mind's eye, my eyes had swollen shut, and I had a cut on my lip. In reality, I had only taken physical damage to my wrists and the back of my head, and I had done that to myself. Yet the scars of what Asphodel had done to me ran deep. I wondered if Lucifer could see them, and I wondered if he appreciated Asphodel's work. He turned to Lethe. "I did it for you, dearest."

His voice was smooth as oil, but Lethe jumped as if he had struck her. "For me? N-no. No! I would never want my Michael chained up and beaten! Never!"

"Oh, I know," said Lucifer. "But you also refused to heed me, and I needed leverage."

Lethe gaped at him, tears turning her pale face red and making strands of white-blond hair stick to her face. "I don't understand."

"I want you to come back to Hell and do your job."

Lethe's head shot up. "Come back?" She shook her head. "No. I'm going to be good, and someday I can go back to Heaven and be with my Michael forever. You can't stop me!"

"Can't I?" A subtle power crept out from Lucifer, reminding everyone there that he was the most powerful being in the room. "I can make you do whatever I want. I'm the most powerful angel in creation." When she shrank away from him, he reined in his presence and held out his hand to her. "But I don't want to do that. Hurting you or forcing you is a resource-intensive strategy that will never win your true loyalty. Torturing Michael, though? Well, that's positively enjoyable."

Lethe froze. "So you're saying you'll let him go if I come back to Hell?"

Lucifer's smile was almost paternal. "Yes, dearest. Come back to Hell and do your job. Control the banshees. Be the properly evil demon I know you can be. And I will let your lover go."

"No!" The word ripped from my throat before I realized it had formed. "Don't do it, Lethe. I'm not worth it. Don't miss out on your chance at salvation."

Salvation. Salvation. Salvation. The word rang in my head like a bell. Cain had once told me she could be my salvation, and in my lighter hours, I had believed her. But in the cave, chained to the wall, only dark hours stretched in front of me. If I left, I didn't know if Cain could save me, but I knew if I stayed, I could save Lethe. My sacrifice would give her a chance to claw her way out of Hell, and with that realization, I felt a calm settle over me.

Tears once more flooded my angel love's eyes, and I didn't need Lucifer's power to know she lacked my certainty. She rocked on her heels, and doubt clouded her eyes.

"Don't you dare choose me, Lethe." My voice was little more than a growl as I pressed my forehead against hers. "Don't you dare." She met my gaze then, her dark demon eyes at odds with her pale complexion, and I knew I had lost this battle.

For the briefest second, I thought maybe such a sacrifice would be enough. Maybe giving up her own chance at Heaven to save me was an act of love great enough to warrant her return to Heaven. But her hardened countenance told me all I needed to know. She wasn't choosing to return to her role as an archdemon only to save me. She also knew that evil was so much easier than redemption.

I should have been disappointed in that moment, but I found myself feeling a kinship with her I hadn't felt in years. I understood so well the desire to do what was easy instead of what was right. Did I not listen to Jophiel instead of fighting with him? Had I not condemned my fellows at the command of my God without even considering my own conscience? Was I not, in my way, as weak as Lethe?

I looked in her eyes, hoping to see the connection I felt with her reflected back at me, but I saw only confusion. She had never seen me as the inadequate creature I knew myself to be. She rose onto her toes and brushed her lips against mine, then turned around and walked toward Lucifer. "I will go back. Let him go."

Lucifer cocked his head to the side, reading Lethe's thoughts enough to recognize the sincerity in her words. He snapped his fingers, and the shackles on my wrists fell back against the wall. "Get out of here," Lucifer said to me. "Before I change my mind."

I didn't know the way through the circuitous passages, but I knew Lucifer would not give me directions. I stumbled toward the entrance, not remembering until I almost fell into him that Bedlam had been there the whole time. The former demon had never stayed silent for so long, at least, not in my presence. I met his gaze, determined to put on the strong face of the leader of the host, and was surprised and ashamed to see a bleak pity there.

He cocked his head toward the tunnel. "Come on. I know the way out." I took a deep breath and followed the angel of chaos into the light.

CHAPTER 19

Siren

"**G**ET OUT," I SAID TO the archangel and the warriors who stood in the entrance to the warehouse. My fellow field angels fell into a semi-circle behind me. They had insisted I was not their leader, but if they flanked me and followed my instructions, I wasn't sure how else to present myself. "The work here is done. We don't need you." I sounded confident and scornful, but my tone was another lie that wasn't a lie, the kind more commonly called bravado. If Martyr had asked me what I felt at that moment, I would have confessed I was afraid.

"Fenyx seemed to need one of my light blades." Rachel never would have dared say such a thing directly to Fenyx, but me she had no problem degrading. I questioned whether leadership was the best role for me.

I didn't let her see my doubt. "Yes, and she used it to take out Beelzebub. By the time he rematerializes, his people will be in police custody, and he won't have time to get another scheme going." Gabriel had been looking between the field angels, the unconscious people, and the warehouse, and he looked me in the eye with a surprising amount of grim respect. I thought he might be willing to let the whole thing go.

Rachel, as ever, was a different story. "Police custody? For those who would dare disrupt the sanctity of the birth of Christ?"

"I mean, they were messing with the light-up trees and the presents," said Annie, a tremor in her voice. "Those are pagan rituals. Maybe by interfering with them, they were actually increasing the sanctity."

Rachel snorted. "You know the punishment for complicity with demons. Stand aside and let me exact it."

I had a brilliant argument planned out about how Rachel thought she knew the punishment but that humans had their own laws that were more appropriate to the current circumstances. I didn't get any further than "I know the punishment you think—" before a cool voice interrupted me from behind.

"You heard the lady," said Fenyx. "Stand aside."

I whipped my head around to glare at Fenyx, ready to give her a piece of my mind, too, if she needed it. She gave me a steady look, then flicked her gaze to Gabriel. I understood then. The field angels and I all knew what would happen if I let Rachel and her warriors into the warehouse, but Gabriel didn't. I didn't want fifty-three people, even fifty-three evildoers, to pay the price to set the archangel on a better path, but as I knew better than anyone, the road to truth could be ugly.

I nodded at Fenyx and stepped back into the semicircle, relinquishing my argument. I thought of turning my back on the scene to show I washed my hands of what happened next, knowing if I did, the others would follow suit. In the end, though, I watched, knowing that even the lowest of sinners—which I did not believe these were—deserved a witness to their deaths.

Within seconds, a horde of warrior angels poured into the entryway and slit the throat of each would-be thief. They didn't wield their accustomed light blades, whose wounds caused painless death in humans. By Rachel's standards, such a death would be too good for these people. Instead, the warriors wielded steel daggers, longswords, claymores, and even a few halbers and glaives. Each had a preferred weapon, wielded with expertise. A few of the criminals died in their sleep, but most of them woke when the blade slashed their throats, their screams turning to gurgling as their blood poured out.

I wanted to scream. I wanted to summon my own katana. I wanted to stop them. I did no such thing. I listened to their cries and kept my gaze on the horror on Gabriel's blood-spattered face.

In less than a minute, it was over. The men lay dead and bloody at our feet, and Rachel nodded her satisfaction. She signaled her warriors, who saluted her as one and disappeared. "Let us know if you need us again, Gabriel," Rachel said to the still-stunned archangel. "We're always happy to serve." Then she blinked out as well.

No one moved for the longest thirty seconds of my existence. Then Gabriel teleported over to me, grabbed my arm, and pulled me through the ether to the other side of the warehouse. He stuck his finger in my face. "You knew this was going to happen!"

"Yes," I said, keeping my voice steady. Part of me wanted to apologize for letting this play out, for sacrificing those men so Gabriel could see the monster that Rachel could be, but I could not. But I told myself I wasn't sorry, and that blood was not on my hands.

"You know she would kill them. All those people..." He trailed off, going back into shock for a moment, but then his eyes narrowed, and he focused on me. "You could have saved them, and you didn't."

Could I have? I wasn't sure. With Martyr at my side and Fenyx's light blade, I might have been able to take out Rachel and a good many of her warriors, but I doubt I could have defeated all of them, not when they each had light blades of their own. But I could have at least gone down fighting, instead of giving up.

"Those people, their deaths," Gabriel continued. "This is on you."

My head shot up, and I glared into his angry blue eyes. "No, archangel," I said. "This is on you." He gasped as if I had struck him, and I went on. "I warned you. I told you not to call Rachel in. I tried to explain what would happen if you did. I warned you that you didn't understand everything about the field angels. You went off in an arrogant snit, convinced you knew the best way to handle everything. You didn't, because of your own ignorance. Because I am truth incarnate, and you didn't believe me."

If I thought my dramatic statement would win Gabriel over, I was mistaken. By the time I had finished, he had recovered. "That's your defense? 'I told you so'? People are *dead*, seraph. Their lives mattered. You don't get to brush them all away as some kind of teaching moment."

I opened my mouth to remind him that he had invited murderers to this den, not me, but before I could, Jubiel stuck his head around the pile of boxes closest to us. "I know you two want to argue all day, but can you hear the mundane kind of siren headed this way?" I took a moment to listen, and realized that every ambulance and police car in the greater Chicago area was probably converging on our position. "We've gotta get out of here if we want them to focus on healing some of the criminals instead of questioning us."

Gabriel looked confused. "Healing the criminals? But they're all dead."

Jubiel shook his head. "Have faith, archangel. We have Fenyx on our side. Some of them may yet live."

Gabriel continued gaping at Jubiel, so I reached out and grabbed his hand. He followed me as I teleported to the field angels' pre-arranged meeting spot on a rooftop a few blocks down. I considered dropping him somewhere else along the way, but I figured that would only delay the conversation I didn't want to continue for a few seconds at most.

When we had all arrived, Gabriel looked at Fenyx. "You saved them all."

Fenyx shrugged. "I probably saved some of them." Her grim features darkened. "I wouldn't have needed to save any of them if you had listened to her in the first place." She inclined her head toward me.

Gabriel closed his eyes and flinched, no doubt recalling the slaughter. "I'm sorry."

"Sorry?" Jubiel let out a humorless laugh. "Sorry doesn't save those poor schlubs, archangel. We had it handled. We may not receive orders from on high, but we do our jobs."

"You're right," Gabriel whispered. Then louder, "You're right. I didn't listen. I thought—"

"We know what you thought," said Jubiel. "You don't have to repeat it."

"I just—" Gabriel shook his head, cutting himself off. "I don't know if you can ever forgive me, but I ask you to try."

"We're *angels*," said Annie with a giggle. "We can forgive anything."

"But Jophiel," said Gabriel. "If all his prayers are going nowhere, someone has to do something about it. Someone has to tell Michael."

I snorted. "Somehow I don't see Michael doing anything about Jophiel any time soon. You're welcome to try to talk to him, but listening has never been Michael's strong suit."

"Then what good am I?" said Gabriel, and I couldn't tell whether he spoke to the group or himself.

Martyr clapped Gabriel on the back. "You wanted to be our leader. We can't allow that. We don't have a leader, don't want a leader. But perhaps, if you want, you can be one of us." Martyr winked at me over Gabriel's shoulder.

"On a trial basis," said Fenyx.

"We're Heaven's misfits," said Jubiel. "You've still got a lot to learn, but there may be some hope for you after all."

For the first time since we began the ordeal of seeking out field angels, Gabriel smiled.

CHAPTER 20

Michael

I FOLLOWED BEDLAM OUT OF THE cave. I didn't ask how he knew exactly what turns to make to lead us out into the afternoon sun, and I couldn't have told you if we circled back on our own tracks once, twice, or even a dozen times. I was aching and exhausted, I was lost in every way an angel could be lost. My own hopeless love had turned her back on Heaven for a second time. In my anguish, I longed for a woman I could never love whom, until very recently, I had thought little better than the devil himself. The only way I could get out of this situation was to follow my anathema through an endless trail of tunnels while my body screamed for respite.

Eventually we emerged from the caves, and my eyes squinted into the bright light. I reached out with my angel senses to orient myself, and their sudden return after I wasn't sure how many days without them staggered me. I wanted nothing more than to cease to exist for the foreseeable future, long enough that I could forget everything that had happened, not just in the cavern but for all of my life.

"Michael?" Bedlam snapped his fingers in front of my face, and I realized he must have been calling my name for a while. "Are you okay?"

No, I thought, but I couldn't say that. Not to Bedlam. Not to anyone. I couldn't admit my own weakness, but at the same time, I had no resources to call upon to mask my distress. A lone tear ran down my cheek, and I couldn't summon the muscle control to wipe it away.

Bedlam studied me for a moment, a look of what I decided to call sympathy rather than pity crossing his face. "You had a rough time of it, didn't you? I don't know what Asphodel did to you, but I know he's one sadistic fucker when he wants to be."

"I'm fine," I managed to croak out.

"You are not fine. If you were hair, you'd be so thick and curly that washing you would be a nightmare. You know what I do when I'm not fine?"

Try to destroy the world? I thought, but I didn't say it out loud. Bedlam hadn't tried to destroy the world in a long time, and I didn't have the energy to snipe at him, especially when he was trying, in his roundabout Bedlam way, to help me.

"I go talk to Khet," he said, then he paused, as if waiting for a protest. When it didn't come, he continued, "I know you guys don't get along super well, but she's good at—"

"Okay," I said. I closed my eyes and pictured her brown eyes filled with passion, and then the sounds of her screams as Asphodel mutilated her. *That wasn't real. Neither of those things was real.*

I opened my eyes again, and Bedlam bent over to peer at me. "Do you... need me to take you there?"

I took a deep breath. I hated to ask anything of Bedlam, but I still couldn't orient myself, and I didn't have the energy for pride. I nodded. "Bedlam reached out and took my hand, and I followed him into the spirit realm.

When I reappeared in my solid form, I was in a small bedroom decorated in red, brown, and black. Bedlam eyed me and said, "Asphodel really did a number on you, didn't he?"

I glanced where he was looking and realized the scrapes and bruises on my arms were still there. I realized I was just as exhausted as I had been before I had teleported. I couldn't imagine why my body hadn't emerged as healed and rested as it usually did after I teleported, unless the scars that Asphodel had inflicted on me went soul-deep.

"I'll go get Khet," said Bedlam, and he opened the door and stepped out.

Left alone in the dim room, I collapsed into the bed and curled on my side. I took deep breaths, reminding myself I was finally safe. The room could have been another of Asphodel's tricks, I supposed, and part of me thought I would wonder for the rest of my life if what I saw was just an elaborate scheme of the Prince of Lies. All I could do was go forward, though.

I waited what seemed an interminable time for Cain to arrive, but I had lost all sense of the passage of time. She may have come two minutes or two hours later for all I could tell. She hurried, at any rate, as she flung open the door and rushed to my side. I looked up into her eyes and realized I didn't have to worry any longer about whether my world was a lie. The concern in care in those eyes could only belong to the real Cain. I felt a weight lift off me just from her presence. I would never mistake a phantom for her again. This Cain did not love me and would never kiss me, but she could offer a peace no illusion ever could.

There was a wheeled chair a few feet away, but instead of dragging it over, she sat on the bed beside me and took my hand. "What happened?"

I shook my head. How could I explain everything that had happened to me? *Maybe coming here wasn't the best idea. I can't tell her what I saw.* I looked away from her. Maybe she could understand, but I didn't want to inflict what I had seen on her. I supposed it was too late though. With her power—*Lucifer's power*—she must know everything.

"I don't," she whispered. "Your mind is such a muddle right now. I can't make sense of anything. All I can hear are screams." A look of immense pain crossed her face. "You don't have to tell me anything you don't want to. I just wish I could do something to help you."

"Cain." I spoke her name, my voice filled with a longing and desperation I had never heard from my own throat. She flinched at the word, and I remembered her name was cursed, and I had no business speaking it to her. Or perhaps she reacted because the screams in my head were overwhelming her, as I knew angel thoughts sometimes did. I should tell her I didn't need her, so she would go, and my turmoil would torture her no more.

"Tell me what I can do for you," she whispered. "Anything. Just, let me help you."

I wondered if she meant that. If I asked, would she leave? Would she kiss me as the phantom Cain had done? Would she forgive me for all the pain I had brought her over the millennia? I didn't know, and I didn't have the courage to find out. Instead I said, "Stay with me."

"Of course."

I lay there in silence for I didn't know how long. When my mind tried to wander to the torture, or my responsibilities, or Lethe, I focused once again on the hand in mine. Eventually, I drifted off into a deep sleep.

When I woke, I felt more rested than I had since even before Asphodel had captured me. The wounds on my body had disappeared, and I could place myself in the world again. Cain was gone. I thought of going to look for her, but since I no longer felt exhausted, I wasn't ready to face the desperate need I'd had for her in my darkest moments. I wouldn't avoid her forever, but I needed time, and as ever, I had work to do.

EPILOGUE

Bedlam

AFTER I LEFT MICHAEL IN Khet's guest room, I went out looking for her. I wasn't sure if she'd made it home yet or how much time had passed since I'd left her on the side of the road in Ohio. I was bad at that kind of thing. I also didn't know if she was still mad. So instead of looking for her my usual way, I crept down the hallway, trying to forestall the inevitable as long as possible, even though that's exactly what had gotten me in the doghouse in the first place.

"—would not believe the couple of days I've had." Gabriel's voice came from the kitchen. Khet was probably home, then. Though Gabriel ostensibly lived here, he never came if Khet wasn't here.

"I'd believe a lot of things." Khet's voice was pretty frosty, especially considering she was talking to Gabriel. "Would you actually be willing to tell me about them, or is it a big angel secret?"

To my mind, Khet was one to talk about keeping secrets. This argument between them needed to happen, and I hated to interrupt it. But I was still going to do it.

I stepped into the kitchen, where Gabriel was sitting at one of the island stools, and Khet was grabbing something out of the refrigerator. "I found Michael," I said. "He needs you." Gabriel leapt to his feet, but I shook my head. "Not you. Khet."

Khet appeared surprised but not as flabbergasted as I would have expected. "Where is he?"

I inclined my head toward the hallway. "Guest room."

As she hurried down the hall, Gabriel asked where I had found him, and I filled in the story as best I knew it. Lucifer had made Asphodel torture Michael in hopes of getting Lethe to return to Hell, and the ploy had worked like a charm. I figured Michael could fill in the details or not as he chose. "You're welcome to hang out until Khet's done."

Gabriel gave me an appraising look.

Oh, right. He lives here. I shouldn't be inviting him to stay.

Yeah, but he's never here, and you're here all the time, so...

True. The television is definitely mine at least.

"I have to go," said Gabriel. "I've finally made progress with the field angels, and I don't want to lose that. Besides, I need to check in with Heaven and make sure everything's okay, since Michael is down here."

I shrugged. As long as he didn't ask me to do any of those things, I was happy.

Khet didn't emerge from the guest room for another three hours, and when she did, she had an unreadable look on her face.

I had taken up the stool Gabriel had vacated because it provided the best view of the television. I flicked off the screen and turned to her. "Khetty!"

"Khetty?" She sounded dubious, but she perched on the stool next to me, a wry smile on her face.

"You don't like it? We could go Russian. You could be Khesha."

"That wouldn't end well for you. You don't look a thing like Mick Jagger."

We sat in silence for a few moments, and I started to wonder whether a peanut butter and pickle sandwich on an everything bagel would be sufficiently satisfying. Khet didn't have much food in her house after a road trip, as it turned out.

"We need to talk," she said eventually.

"About how 'Blow' is about a suicide cult?"

"What? No!" Khet shook her head, as if trying to rid herself of my ridiculousness. "Bedlam."

I couldn't read minds, but somehow I knew what she wanted to talk about, and I wasn't looking forward to this particular conversation. "I don't want to talk." I pushed the stool away from the island, ready to go get that bagel after all.

She put her hand on my arm to stop me. "We need to." She took a deep breath. "You know you're my best friend in the whole world. You've been there for me when literally no one else has been. If I had to pick someone to be stranded on a desert island with, it would be you. Which is saying something, because if you were stuck in any one place like that, you would be miserable company. I love you. But I'm not in love with you. And you're not in love with me."

I sighed. "I know. You're right. It's just—"

"It would solve so many problems? I know. But you'll find the right person for you someday, and I have Gabriel."

I turned on my Azrael-love-vision and looked at her again. "Gabriel's fading."

"I know." Translation: "I don't want to talk about it."

I looked at the shadow I still couldn't quite make out behind her. "There's someone else."

"I know. It's not you. Don't worry about it." She *really* didn't want to talk about it.

"You know, Khet, all that advice you gave me about falling in love with a human could just as easily apply to you. You're just as immortal as me, and—"

"I *know*, Bedlam." The bite in her words was enough to make me stop. I didn't want her mad at me again. "I told you it's fine. I'm not leaving Gabriel."

"But if you don't love him—"

"I do love him. He's just... never here, and when he is... I dunno. I think we both loved the idea of each other more than the reality. But I can't do to him what Keziel did to you."

"That's different," I said with resolution.

Khet smiled at that. "How is it different?"

Because Keziel really loved me...

Because Keziel loved me and left me...

"Because I like you better than I like Gabriel."

She laughed, then got up and opened the refrigerator. "Is there any food in this place?"

I grinned at her. "I wouldn't say no to a pizza."

She opened up her laptop and put in the website for Luigi's. "Pineapple and anchovies it is."

THANK YOU!

Thank you so much for reading the Earthbound Angels series. I hope you enjoyed *Angel in the Details,* despite all the times Bedlam screwed up. If you want to keep up with news on my upcoming books, follow Elizabeth Corrigan, Author on Facebook or look for me on BookBub. If you enjoyed the book (or honestly, even if you didn't), I would love for you to leave a review on Amazon, Goodreads, and/or BookBub. Regardless of whether you do any of these things, I appreciate all my readers and hopefully won't keep you waiting too long for the next installment!

CHECK OUT THE OTHER BOOKS IN THE EARTHBOUND ANGELS SERIES!

Oracle of Philadelphia, Earthbound Angels Book 1

Carrie works at a diner in South Philadelphia, dispensing advice to humans and angels wise enough to seek her counsel. But there are some problems that even the best advice can't solve.

Her latest supplicant, Sebastian, is unique among those who have sought her aid. He sold his soul to a demon in exchange for his sister's life, but his heart remains pure.

Carrie has lived for millennia with the knowledge that her immortality is due to the suffering of others, and she cannot bear to see another good man damned when it is within her power to prevent it.

In order to renegotiate his contract, Carrie must travel into the depths of hell and parley with the demons that control its pathways. As the cost of her journey rises, Carrie must determine how much she is willing to sacrifice to save one good soul.

Raising Chaos, Earthbound Angels Book 2

When good fails, chaos rises to the challenge.

The daily life of a chaos demon is delightfully sinful—overindulging in Sri Lankan delicacies, trespassing on private beaches in Hawaii, and getting soused at the best angel bar on the planet. But when Bedlam learns that the archdemon Azrael has escaped from the Abyss in order to wreak vengeance against the person who sent her there—Bedlam's best friend, Khet—he can't sit idly by.

Only one relic possesses the power to kill Khet, who suffers immortality at Lucifer's request: the mythical Spear of Destiny, which pierced Christ's side at His crucifixion. Neither angel nor demon has seen the Spear in two thousand years, but Azrael claims to know its location. Bedlam has no choice but to interpret woefully outdated clues and race her to its ancient resting place.

His quest is made nearly impossible by the interference of a persnickety archivist, Keziel—his angelic ex—and a dedicated cult intent on keeping the Spear out of the wrong hands. But to Bedlam, "wrong" is just an arbitrary word, and there's no way he's letting Khet die without a fight.

Archangel Errant, Earthbound Angels Book 3

Divine intervention isn't all it's cracked up to be.

Gabriel didn't expect his return to Heaven to be filled with trumpets and celebration, but he thought he would do more than sit at Michael's side, listening to endless catalogs of unfulfilled prayers. He's tried blending into every aspect of Heavenly life, but he can't help but feel that the constantly praying Faithful and flower-dispensing Handmaidens lack the motivation to do any true good in the world. Some days, he longs for nothing more than to return to Earth and tell his beloved Cassia how he feels about her.

When Heaven is suddenly attacked, all the angels become trapped in their own nightmares. With Michael gone on an angelic mission, Gabriel must rally the remaining seraphim to rouse the sleeping angels and discover who seeks to take the agents of Heaven out of the celestial battle. All fingers point to Bedlam, but Gabriel can't believe the ex-demon would threaten his salvation so soon after gaining it.

With few people he trusts, Gabriel must rely on all the lessons he learned on Earth to save Heaven, Bedlam, and maybe even himself.

Carrie, Khet, Cassia, Cama, Cain. She's had hundreds of names through the centuries. Now she's Chloe, an ordinary college student—at least as ordinary as a mind-reader can be when she has an angel for a boyfriend and a best friend who often forgets he's not still a demon.

When Chloe discovers a fellow student has been murdered, she's determined to stay out of it. Much as she wants to help, interfering has gotten her nothing but trouble in the past, and she needs to stick it out at the university for at least four years if she wants her degree. But when she inadvertently gives away her power at the funeral, she finds she has no choice but to use her unique gifts to track down the killer.

Check out the Valeriel Investigations series by Elizabeth Corrigan

Catching a Man, Valeriel Investigations Book 1

Kadin Stone's life is finally going according to plan. She's starting her new job as a homicide detective's aide at one of the premier criminal investigation companies in Valeriel City, the capital of a 1950's-style kingdom. Kadin is certain her new position will introduce her to any number of eligible men, so she'll finally be able to get married and stop burdening the brother who insists on supporting her.

On Kadin's first day, the royal family calls in her team to investigate the murder of gossip-rag cover girl Queen Callista. Kadin's superiors think it's an open and shut case. The queen's jilted lover Duke Baurus DeValeriel had motive, means, and opportunity, but Kadin can't help but spot holes in their theory.

After checking into a few leads of her own, Kadin inadvertently ends up in the confidence of Duke Baurus. When she tries to share what she knows with the rest of the team, she finds them unwilling to listen to the opinion of a girl who they know is only after a ring on her finger. In order to see justice served, Kadin finds herself doing the last thing she expected when she started working for a homicide detective—solve a murder!

Staying on Top, Valeriel Investigations Book 2

Kadin Stone should be over the moon—or at least one of the two moons that grace the sky of Valeriel City. She has a great job working as an aide for one of the best homicide detectives in the city, and her boyfriend is on the verge of proposing. Getting married means she'll have to give up her day job, but wedding bells have been her life goal for as long as she can remember. But she's not happy, and she can't quite figure out why.

Until Duke Baurus DeValeriel walks back into her life.

Kadin cleared Baurus of a murder charge six months ago, and she thought that was the last she'd see of him. After all, they move in completely different circles. But Baurus has need of a homicide detective after a rising film star dies at one of his parties. He's convinced Kadin is the only one who can solve the case. Kadin's only too happy to lend her expertise, but as the case progresses, she gets the feeling that Baurus wants more from her, and she's not sure what she has to offer.

As the case leads Kadin from one tawdry secret to another—secrets only she seems capable of uncovering—she questions whether marriage is what she wants out of life. But it's not always easy to decide whether to follow your dreams or follow your heart.

Check out the Transients series by Elizabeth Corrigan

Arachne's Web, Transients Book 1
Seven Strangers

Three Students: Bliss Bhanushali feels an instant connection to her roommate Lexi and Lexi's boyfriend Will, though both girls can't help but feel Will is keeping something from them.

Two Scoundrels: Jack and Cobalt Zhao find themselves on the run after their foolproof plan to rob a space train goes inexplicably awry.

A Soldier: Gavin Ibori must fight for his very survival in a challenge designed to test the mettle of the most promising new warriors.

A Servant: Roslyn Turin wants nothing more than her freedom, but her dreams of another life send her into psychiatric care instead.

One History

By day, they are seven strangers from different moons. At night, they dream of their interconnected lives twenty years ago. Their visions send them to the mysterious moon of Arachne, where an archaeological dig turns up strange alien artifacts.

Then the dreams get darker, filled with images of glowing symbols and spattered blood.

In their last lives, they were murdered. And if they don't find out why, history is doomed to repeat itself.

ABOUT ELIZABETH CORRIGAN

Elizabeth has degrees in English and psychology and has spent several years working as a data analyst in various branches of the healthcare industry. When she's not hard at work on her next novel, Elizabeth enjoys singing, reading teen vampire novels, and making Sims of her characters.

She drinks more Diet Coke than is probably optimal for the human body and is pathologically afraid of bees. She lives in Maryland with two cats and a purple Smart Car.

www.ingramcontent.com/pod-product-compliance
Lightning Source LLC
Chambersburg PA
CBHW051918240626
47153CB00004B/1273